D1615772

STUDIO CHIZU'S

BELLE

MAMORU HOSODA

STUDIO CHIZU'S
BELLE

MAMORU HOSODA

Translation by WINIFRED BIRD
English lyrics by LUDVIG FORSSELL

Yen On
150 West 30th Street, 19th Floor
New York, NY 10001

Visit us at yenpress.com • facebook.com/yenpress
twitter.com/yenpress • yenpress.tumblr.com
instagram.com/yenpress

First Yen On Edition: September 2023
Edited by Yen On Editorial: Rachel Mimms
Designed by Yen Press Design: Wendy Chan

Yen On is an imprint of Yen Press, LLC.
The Yen On name and logo are trademarks of Yen Press, LLC.

The publisher is not responsible for websites (or their content) that are not owned by the publisher.

Library of Congress Cataloging-in-Publication Data
Names: Hosoda, Mamoru, 1967- author. |
Bird, Winifred, translator. |
Studio Chizu (Production company)
Title: Studio Chizu's Belle / Mamoru Hosoda ;
translation by Winifred Bird
Other titles: Belle
Description: First Yen On edition. | New York, NY :
Yen On, 2022.
Identifiers: LCCN 2022030834 | ISBN 9781975350956
(hardcover)
Subjects: CYAC: Science fiction. | Fantasy. |
Online identities—Fiction. |
Celebrities—Fiction. | Identity—Fiction. |
LCGFT: Science fiction. |
Fantasy fiction. | Light novels.
Classification: LCC PZ7.7.H68 S78 2022 |
DDC 895.63/6—dc23/eng/20220705
LC record available at https://lccn.loc.gov/2022030834

ISBNs: 978-1-9753-5095-6 (hardcover)
978-1-9753-5096-3 (ebook)

10 9 8 7 6 5 4 3 2 1

LSC-C

Printed in the United States of America

AN INVITATION

A streak of white emerges from the darkness.

Slowly, it approaches.

What is it?

Gradually, it comes into focus. It's a string of intricately detailed units. Like cells viewed beneath a microscope, one follows the next in an orderly procession.

Cells?

No—it's a city.

The enigmatic megalopolis called U.

The ultimate virtual world, created by the Voices, the five sages who preside over the wisdom of this universe.

The biggest online space in history, with more than five billion users worldwide and counting.

You're still not on U.

How do you access it?

Take out your phone. You'll see the U icon on the home screen. Most smartphones have it pre-installed, so you can use it right away.

Start up the app.

U will be you.

You will be U.

U will be everything.

Any smart devices you're currently wearing—earphones, wristwatches, earrings, rings, glasses, fake nails, masks, whatever—will automatically scan your personal data.

Reading your biometric information...

While the app authenticates you—it won't take long—U's membership policy is displayed. Next comes a slate of icons representing different people. Icons of all ages, genders, shapes, and handicaps are juxtaposed with Us written in different ways.

"Much like the differences and particularities that make each person in the world unique, this image explores a variety of differently shaped U particles to embody this ethos."

From this infinite variety of Us, one is selected.

Authentication is now complete.

"Welcome to the world of U."

The chosen U flies through an infinite corridor of smartphone-shaped windows.

This is the authenticated you.

The U transforms into a cute rabbit-girl.

An announcement echoes from the screen.

"U utilizes the latest in body-sharing technology that allows everyone to relax and enjoy their time together."

In this world, avatars are called ASes, short for "autonomous selves." Your AS is your double in U. It is automatically created using U's cutting-edge AI technology to process your scanned biometric information.

See all the ASes flying through the windows? They're being generated from U particles as users log in, just like you did.

You—that is, the adorable young girl with fluffy white ears

poking out of her stylish hat—and the friends you've just met are skydiving downward.

Suddenly, the sea of clouds filling your vision clears.

The skyscrapers reflecting the twilight sun are enough to make you gasp in awe.

The elaborately constructed geometric clusters of buildings overlap one another in every direction, creating a sunset vista unlike any you've ever seen.

Strolling through the luxurious shopping malls, you feel as free as if you've been let off work while it's still light out to wander the Champs-Élysées or Fifth Avenue or Ginza. Simply watching all the ASes decked out in a rainbow of colors feels like attending a masked ball in Venice.

Graphical representations of flowers come fluttering down like confetti. You pick one up and smell it. Within the lush, sensual scent lurks one that is fresher, more youthful. It's perfect for this city.

Suddenly, as you flit down the lively avenue, you look up. Where the sky should be are upside-down skyscrapers, so tightly packed they look ready to tumble down upon you. Carved out in the middle of them is a park where you can watch ASes frolicking happily.

How can a city make you feel so free?

You know with your whole being that this is the center of the world.

You glimpse the moon between the skyscrapers.

Another announcement plays from the screen.

"U is another reality. Your AS is another you. Everything is here."

The crescent moon is tipped on its side in imitation of a U.

"You can't redo life in the real world. But in U, you can. It's time to live as another you. It's time to begin a new life. It's time to change the world."

Suddenly, the whole city goes quiet.

A song.

Someone is singing.

Where is the sound coming from? Multitudes of ASes look around, searching for the source. You, too, perk up your long white ears.

The song is grand and delicate at the same time. Intimate but also powerful.

You can't help being pulled in.

"Over there!" someone shouts.

Multitudes of AS eyes focus on a single point.

A whale.

An enormous whale covered in countless speakers floats leisurely between the upside-down buildings. You make out a small figure wearing a crimson dress standing on the tip of the whale's rostrum. That's where the song seems to be coming from.

A roar emanates from the speakers encrusting the whale's body.

The girl stands motionless on the rostrum, singing with a voice so powerful it holds its own against the surging accompaniment.

What looked at first like a crimson dress is actually a garment composed of dahlias, gerbera daisies, poppy anemones, echinacea, and other flowers in countless shades of red.

Her long hair is an unreal pink color.

Her eyes are as blue and deep as the sea.

A truly matchless beauty.

Dotting her cheeks are what appear to be freckles.

"Belle!"

"It's Belle!"

The ASes stare up at her, crying her name:
Belle.

lalalai
lalalai

When our heartbeats collide,
I won't mind, in a place we've never been before;
I'm reaching out for the moon
and stars beyond it

lalalai
lalalai

Is it you I will find?
Though I feel left behind sometimes when you
close the door
I wanna know who you are, I wanna know it all

The moment that life hits you,
you can't avoid the issue
You're disconnected from the world you thought
you were a part of

But if you close your eyes and let go
of that mirage you haven't met,
nobody else decides the words you see in your heart

So, line up, the party's over here
Come one, come all, jump into the fire

Step up, we are whatever we wanna be,
we are free, that's all we desire

When you pass through the veil of fantasy
There's a world with a rhythm for you and me

"Belle!"

"Belle!!"

"Belle!!"

Among the multitude of voices calling her name is your own. Without realizing it, you are singing her song. She smiles down on the cheering masses. For an instant, you think your eyes meet hers, and a warmth envelops your chest. You are drawn to her from the moment you see her. You can't take your eyes away.

You've only just met, but you are her captive.

"Belle!"

"Belle!!"

"Belle!"

"Belle!!"

She crosses her arms over her chest and then flings them open.

At the same moment, graphical images of flowers burst from her body. The flowers drift onto the city from above the placidly floating whale.

She belts out her song as if she is blessing all people, all things, all life.

Who in the world is she?

SUZU

"Bwah!"

I thrust aside my thin blanket and sat up, gasping for breath. My head almost banged into the low ceiling; the rafters of this shabby, rustic attic sloped down right over my bed.

"Haaah, haaah... Haaah..."

It was morning. The sunlight was blinding.

The brilliant world I'd just waken from still lingered so fresh in my mind. I closed my eyes, reaching for its dregs. I'd been standing on that whale's rostrum, singing. I was wearing fancy clothes, belting my heart out.

I opened my eyes again. My phone was lying on the sheets, its screen blank. I could see myself reflected in its dark surface, lit up by the sun. I was wearing the same frumpy, faded pajamas I'd had since junior high. My hair was sticking up in various places, my eyes half closed.

And spattered over my cheeks—were freckles.

They made me so depressed. My chest felt tight; I let slip a sigh.

"Phew..."

Immediately, I heard Dad call from downstairs.

"Suzu? What's wrong?"

Panic set in.

Did he hear me just now? Needless to say, my room isn't a soundproof booth. It's just the ordinary room of a miserable seventeen-year-old girl. The only way to keep people from hearing stuff is to curl up in a ball under the blankets. *Did I sigh more loudly than usual...?* I felt a surge of regret, and my back broke out in a cold sweat.

"Nothing! I'm fine...!!" I hurriedly shouted back, crouched on all fours on my bed.

What do I do if he comes upstairs to check on me? I mean, he probably won't. But what if—?

"Oops—"

My hand slipped, and I collapsed face-first onto the floor.

I changed into my school uniform and went downstairs. Dad was nowhere to be seen. He must have been getting ready for work.

I opened the porch door to let Fugue out and the cool morning air in. I gave the living and dining rooms a quick sweep and stacked the magazines scattered on the table. While I waited for the kettle to boil, I picked some flowers from the garden, stuck them in a vase, and set it next to a framed photo in the kitchen. Then I put a teabag in my mug and poured in the water, sending the steamy scent of black tea swirling upward. Mom was smiling at me in the photo, just like she always did.

Fugue was waiting eagerly in the garden, so I gave him some food. From a distance, the tan flecks in his white fur made him look dingy, like the poor dog never got a bath.

He lost his front right paw in an accident where he got it caught in a wild boar trap someone put out. The pink stump stuck out as he ate, making him wobble around like he was about to fall over. People must have really felt sorry for him before we adopted him.

I sat on the porch and sipped my tea, staring at Fugue.

Dad walked out to the garage. He was wearing a navy T-shirt over his tan skin, his backpack full of work gear draped over one shoulder.

"Want a ride?" he asked me.

I kept staring at Fugue, my mug covering my mouth.

"...No thanks," I replied.

"What about dinner?"

"No thanks."

"...Okay. Well, see you later."

I bet he was frowning. I can tell without looking at him.

I heard the engine of his little four-wheel-drive start. He backed up, swerved into the road, and drove down the hill. The sound of gravel crunching under the tires faded away.

I'm not sure when I stopped being able to look him in the eye. Or how long since we had a real conversation. Or how much time has passed since we ate a meal together.

A notification pinged on my phone. There was a text bubble on the screen:

Belle is the most beautiful woman in all of U

Languages from all over the world were translated instantaneously.

Her music is super unique

Belle's songs are bursting with confidence

The hottest account out of all 5 billion users

Text bubbles popped up one after another, filling the space around Belle's icon in seconds.

But they didn't make me feel happy or accomplished or elated. No matter how much attention Belle got, it didn't affect me. I huddled in my shell, my lips resting on the chipped rim of the mug.

One of the text bubbles swelled larger, which was what happened to comments getting the most attention.

Out of all the countless comments at that moment, this one was generating the biggest buzz:

Who in the world is Belle?

Fugue gave me a puzzled look.

He seemed concerned that I was acting so depressed.

Most people probably don't know this, but Kochi Prefecture here on the island of Shikoku is actually a gorgeous, fertile place covered in steep mountains threaded with sparkling blue streams. Lots of the people who revolutionized Japan's feudal society more than a hundred and fifty years ago came from here, which is something else we're proud of. Plus we have the sunniest weather nationwide. And the highest alcohol consumption per person. Maybe that's why folks here are supposedly so laid-back and friendly and cheerful. Granted, we've still got some pessimistic sad sacks.

Like me.

My home is on the edge of a village of about thirty houses dotted over the side of a mountain. Down below there's a river called the Niyodo, with the Chinka Bridge connecting us to the other side. It was built without any railings so that it wouldn't wash away during a flood. And as long as there isn't a flood, I cross it every day. Today the Niyodo was quiet and blue.

Sometimes tourists come in their rental cars and stand on the bridge taking pictures and oohing and aahing about how pretty and blue it is. *What a sweet little village*, they say as they strike a pose for the camera. They don't know anything about this place.

I climbed down the stone stairs with my schoolbag under my arm and walked down the steep road, my loafers slapping the asphalt. Neighborhood housewives used to say hello to me and wish me a good day at school while they swept their front stoops. That doesn't happen anymore. On a lot of the houses, the rain shutters are closed tight. Some of the people have passed away, and some have moved to the city. Every year there are fewer of us. Lots of villages are like that in the Niyodo watershed. I heard that the sociologist who invented the phrase "disappearing village" in the nineties based it on a place near here. I can't tell you how many times in my life I've heard adults say, "You'd be surprised how many people used to live here in the old days." We're at the cutting edge of population loss, falling birth rates, and an aging society. That's the cold, hard truth.

Once I climb the road on the other side of the river and come out on the highway, there's a bus stop. The schedule in its rusted frame only lists buses that run in the morning and evening. If you miss the bus, you're out of luck.

After a few minutes, the bus came. I took my usual seat in the back. I was the only passenger. We passed a bunch of stops without anyone getting on. I stared at the signboard next to the driver's seat as we bumped along.

THIS ROUTE WILL BE DISCONTINUED AT THE END OF SEPTEMBER.

I live in a place where at some point no one else is going to live. I'm standing on the edge of a cliff next to the raging ocean. I feel like I'm at the end of the world, with nothing more left and no one to depend on.

I got off the bus, passed through the ticket gate at JR Ino Station, and boarded the train (technically a diesel locomotive) waiting by the platform. The floor of the nearly empty train car shimmered under the morning light. At each stop, more kids wearing uniforms from different junior high and high schools got on. The closer we got to downtown, the smaller the patch of light on the floor shrank and the more the people packed into the two-car train. Then the conductor announced the name of my station.

I joined the stream of kids wearing the same uniform on the road to school, and we climbed the gentle hill together. I'm one of them. That thought reassures me.

The summer sun was bright and blinding.

Last fall, the brass band was giving a performance in front of the school tree in the courtyard. Lots of students were gathered around listening.

Brass band shows are always popular. They don't just play music; the members march along to the songs. They put on a fun, energetic show. All the instruments play perfectly in time with the marching, and they never mess up or go offbeat.

Me and Hiro—full name Hiroka Betsuyaku—were listening from the second-floor gym's veranda.

When the band started the second song, a tall, slender girl stepped out in front with her alto sax. Then she played a perfect solo, her long wavy hair swaying as she stepped briskly back and forth.

"...She's so pretty," I blurted out.

Ruka—full name Ruka Watanabe—had the kind of vivid beauty that captivates you whether you like it or not. I heard some other girls on the veranda talking about her.

"She's, like, the most popular girl in school."

"Her legs are so long and thin."

"She looks like a model, even in her uniform."

"Seriously!"

They nodded at each other.

"They're just jealous because their legs aren't long or thin," Hiro said to me softly, so they couldn't hear, turning a page in her book. The girls kept talking.

"Ruka is such a natural leader."

"People gravitate to her like she's the sun in their universe."

Hiro frowned behind her silver-rimmed glasses.

"That must be so annoying," she said. "In that sense, you have it easy, Suzu. You're like the dark side of the moon; everyone stays away from you."

I choked on the air and looked at her, aghast.

"H-Hiro."

"What?"

"You think you could take the harshness down a notch?"

"Harsh? Me?"

Just then, a loud voice interrupted the performance.

"Join the canoe club!"

Everyone looked toward the voice.

"It's Kamishin!"

"Kamishin's here!"

Kamishin—full name, Shinjiro Chikami—was recruiting people at random, a paddle in his hand and a sign reading CANOE on his back.

"How about you? Wanna join the club?"

"Cut it out, Kamishin!"

"No way!"

The two older boys ran away laughing. Kamishin chased them for a minute, then spun around to confront a group of girls.

"Well, ladies? Up for some canoeing?"

"Eeeek!"

The girls screamed in genuine horror and ran away.

"Or you? Wanna give it a try?"

"Run, he's coming!"

He was serious enough, but everyone else's reaction made him seem crazy. He looked like a wild beast flailing in a crowd of beautiful girls.

"Lemme tell you about the canoe club—"

"Ahhhh!"

As I watched them run from him, I felt an urge to defend his earnestness.

"It's pretty amazing that he started that club by himself," I said to Hiro.

"He's the only member, though," she replied.

"I wonder why..."

"Why? Obviously—"

Hiro paused, looking toward Ruka, who was playing on distractedly. Her back was turned on Kamishin and her posture was stiff, like she didn't want to look at him. Hiro noticed it, sure enough. She slammed her book shut and scowled at Ruka.

"—because everyone thinks he's a joke, to put it mildly."

We left the gym and wandered through the school building. The chorus club, the biology club, the band, the dance club...they were all recruiting members. As we crossed the glassed-in breezeway, I heard girls shouting and clapping.

A one-on-one basketball game was going on outside—an exhibition performance by the boys' basketball team. Someone tossed the ball onto the court for the next game, and a boy in a hoodie caught it deftly.

"Oh..."

It was Shinobu.

The game started. Shinobu—full name, Shinobu Hisatake—dribbled it slowly, checking out his opponent, an older boy. The opponent had his knees bent and his arms out to guard against a jump shot. Shinobu tried to dribble around him but then retreated, repelled by his defense.

With a sudden, efficient motion, he made a jump shot.

Man, he was fast.

His opponent spread his arms over his head but missed the ball by a hair. Shinobu's earlier attempt had been a feint. The ball arced cleanly through the air and through the hoop.

The row of girls watching from the third-floor hallway erupted in giddy applause. Shinobu didn't even crack a smile. That cool attitude was what drove the girls wild.

Before the clapping stopped, the next game had begun. *Bounce, bounce, bounce.* Shinobu waited for the right moment, then dribbled low past his opponent, like he was showing off his strength. Driving past in a flash, he landed a layup. The ball made a pleasing sound as it slipped through the net.

Applause echoed off the walls again.

"...I can't believe how tall Shinobu got," I mumbled to Hiro, like I was talking to myself.

"Didn't you say you were friends when you were little?"

"*Ahem*. Actually, he proposed to me once."

"Seriously? Like how?"

"'Suzu, I'll protect you.'"

"How old were you?"

"Six."

"...Okay, that was ages ago." Hiro sighed. It sounded like she'd had enough of me.

Shinobu made another basket. The game ended with more applause. He exited the court next to his opponent, stone-faced.

My old friend Shinobu.

He was no longer within my reach.

After school, I plodded across the Chinka Bridge.

Shinobu and I went to nursery school and elementary school together. After that he moved to the city and we didn't see each other anymore. We reunited in high school, but things weren't the same.

Back then, I never thought I'd turn into one of those kids who's always looking down at their feet. But there's a reason I'm like this.

I watched the Niyodo flow placidly by.

It happened a long time ago.

A white bird skimmed over the water's surface.

MEMORIES

"Mommy?"

"What, Suzu?" she answered, looking back at me.

It was eleven years ago. Our house was still new. We didn't have a garage yet, and potted flowers lined the yard.

"I'm not cutting my hair."

I ran down the hill in front of the house. Mom ran down the stairs on the other side, circled around, and waited for me with her hands on her hips. I hopped away, shouting that I would never ever get a haircut. But she dragged me back mercilessly, sat me down on the garden bench, and tied the salon cape over my shoulders.

"You're going to look so cute," she said. Ugh. I hated how the freshly cut ends pricked my skin. She was cutting it above my shoulders because "you're going to be an elementary student now." Soon my bangs were way high over my eyebrows. My neck kept itching for a while even after I started school.

I used to play with Mom a lot. We wrestled on the grassy riverbank in the evenings. I would push her as hard as I could, and she would roll over in the grass.

"I won!" I smiled happily. She smiled, too.

I asked her why. "Is it 'cause I'll cry if I lose?"

She shook her head. "I'm happy my delicate little Suzu is so strong now." Dad lay in the grass, smiling as he watched us.

Mom made *katsuo tataki* a lot. She would salt pieces of the fish and thread it onto metal skewers, then blister it right over the flame, skin side first. I would stand on a chair and watch. She patted the dripping fat off with paper towels so the stovetop didn't get dirty. When the red flesh turned pale, she dunked it in ice water, pulled it off, and patted it dry. She always cut it into super fat chunks. I was just a little kid, so I could hardly pick the huge pieces up with my chopsticks, let alone fit them in my mouth. She would sit there, mug in hand, watching me struggle as she waited for Dad to come home. Back then Dad worked in an office and wore a necktie every day.

Maybe that's why we had a little more money in those days. Mom bought the newest model of phone. We wanted to test out the camera, so I sat on Dad's lap and pointed the phone at her. He helped me get her in the frame before I pressed the shutter. She was so pretty, smiling in her white clothes. We printed the picture out, and we still have it at home.

Unlike now, I was an energetic kid who used to run all over the place. I much preferred playing outside to being indoors. If there was a tree, I climbed it. If there was grass, I ripped it up. If there was a bug, I chased it. But I never got sunburned. It must have been in my genes. Instead, freckles covered my face. Scrapes and scars covered my knees. I used to trip over my feet in the woods and on the riverbanks and the hill outside the house. Mom would come running and hug me tight while I cried. Magically, the pain would go away. I was so happy back then. I don't know how many times I fell down because I loved playing and I wanted Mom to hug me. She'd always come running like it was the most serious matter in the world.

Every day was like summer vacation. I followed Mom around while she did the laundry and cleaned the house. After lunch, we would throw open the living-room doors, lay down quilts on the floor, and take a nap together. Incense swirled through the air to keep the mosquitoes away. When I opened my eyes, Mom was usually not where I expected her to be, but instead busily doing housework. When I think back on it, she never once told me she was too busy. Any time I asked for her, she gave me her full attention.

Since we lived in the mountains, we never went out to eat. Instead, Mom would cook us whatever we wanted. One day, I told her I wanted to eat yakitori like I'd seen in a picture book. I'd never had it before. She made it for me, skewering each piece of chicken and grilling it. For the first time in my life, I saw real yakitori. Not knowing how to eat it, I had trouble pulling the meat off the skewers with my teeth. Mom and Dad just stared at me, like they didn't want to miss the chance to see me do something for the first time.

Living in the mountains, we didn't go to amusement parks or shopping malls for fun; we'd just go further into the mountains to a campsite. On sunny summer days, Mom and I donned broad-brimmed hats and crossed the Chinka Bridge. Dad always carried all the camp gear.

The crystal pools at the far end of Yasui Gorge were so blue they left even us locals speechless. The water was so clear we could see our own shadows at the bottom of the river. Swimming in the river felt like being in midair, which scared me a little.

Mom was an excellent swimmer. She told me proudly that when she was growing up, she used to swim in these crystal pools every day in summer, like a water imp. She knew all the joy the river could give. But she never swam anywhere dangerous when the weather was bad, and she never let me do that, either. She used to circle around me as I floated in my inner tube and then plunge downward, showing off. Stuck in my tube, I'd get frightened and call for her: "*Mommy, don't go!*" But she would swim off through the blue water like she couldn't hear me.

One evening, I was playing with Mom's phone when I found a weird app. When I started it up, black and white stripes appeared. I asked Dad what it was. He stared at it, gave me a puzzled look, and called Mom from the kitchen where she was making dinner. After dinner, Mom took the phone and turned it sideways. I realized the stripes were the keys of a piano. At her urging, I pressed one. A "do" played.

"It played!" I said, looking at Mom.

"It did," she said, looking back at me. It was an app she used to compose music.

For the first time, I looked around Mom's room and noticed that the shelves were packed with old records and cassette tapes and CDs. I realized that when she put one of them on the record player or tape deck connected to an amp, music played from the speakers on either side. Her collection hit on all the key points in the history of classical, jazz, and rock music history. I had no idea back then of how much value and meaning this fabulous collection had, being in a house in the middle of nowhere.

In that room, I played the keyboard app over and over, recording the notes. When I pressed play, they sang back to me in order. No matter how outrageous the tune I tapped in, the app played it back faithfully. It made me so overwhelmingly happy I jumped up and down on my chair. Mom smiled, too, her face glowing under the warm light of the incandescent bulb.

From that day on, I was obsessed with the app. I would beg Mom for her phone and play with it morning, noon, and night. It was intuitive and easy to use. Since it wasn't designed for children, there were lots of words I couldn't read and functions I didn't understand. But I didn't care. I couldn't get enough of this exciting new experience of creating music. I wrote countless songs, demoing them all for Mom. After hearing each one, she would give me a few words of advice: *Do this and it will be even better. The trick is this.* Sometimes she would pull out some of her records and play them for me as inspiration. Mom wasn't a professional musician or songwriter, but when I think back on her advice, all of it was spot-on. One time, I remember her listening to one of my melodies and saying "Oh!" as if she'd noticed something, then singing it back to herself softly.

"What do you think?" I asked.

"Not bad," she said.

According to her, she'd been watching nervously as I composed it. I was putting notes in places they normally wouldn't go. She was sure this song would be a failure and all my hard work up till then would be for nothing. But as it took shape, she said it mysteriously came together in a good way. I was so overjoyed I wanted to roll around on the floor in celebration. Even when she admitted that she was probably listening with a mother's biased ear, I still felt happy. I wasn't writing music for some stranger to listen to. All I cared about was that Mom listened to it. She sang out my melody, tapping the beat with her right hand. She sang so beautifully, too. She used to have a singing group with her friends, and her voice was clear and free. She sang my weird little song for me over and over. I was so happy, I sang along with her, although somehow my voice didn't sound as amazing as hers.

That's where my happy memories of Mom abruptly end.

August came.

All the memories after that are horrible and painful.

* * *

The cries of a little girl echoed over the river.

She was stuck all by herself on a sandbank.

I'd say she was four or five. She looked younger than me.

It had been so sunny a minute earlier, but all of a sudden, heavy clouds blanketed the sky. I'd looked away from the pretty, peaceful river for what felt like a few minutes, and when I looked back, it was a muddy, swollen swirl sweeping branches away with astounding speed. There must've been a rainstorm somewhere upstream.

Earlier that day, when the water was still clear, a group of people had been shouting happily on the opposite bank. Now they were on the same side as us, staring blankly at the little girl. I could tell right away from their colorful outfits that they were from the city. The little girl, too, was wearing clothes brighter than anything I was used to. How could those people from the city have lost track of a little girl wearing such a bright outfit? How could they have forgotten her when they came back to this side of the river?

All the people hanging out by the river, canoeing and fishing with their friends and family, were standing there like statues, like there was nothing they could do. In a way, it made sense. That's how violent the river separating us from the little girl had become. Everyone understood that rescuing her wouldn't be easy. One of the adults was talking to someone on their cell phone, but all of us could see the sandbank steadily shrinking; we knew that no emergency crew would ever make it on time. That's why we were standing there so helplessly.

Was our only choice to stand here and listen to the little girl cry?

Just then, someone grabbed a red life jacket from a canoe and stepped forward, pulling it on without taking her eyes off the stranded child.

It was Mom.

"Mommy!" I cried, desperately clutching the hem of her shirt. I could tell she was about to do something really dangerous. Fear overwhelmed me. I pulled on her as hard as I could, screaming her name, trying to hold her back. She squatted down and squeezed my hand and told me something; I can't remember what. Maybe I couldn't hear her because I was wailing so loudly.

She stood up, shook me off, and ran toward the water, buckling the life jacket as she went. I tried to chase her but stumbled on the rocky riverbank and fell. Still, I got back up and screamed after her.

"Don't go!"

I don't think she heard me. She ran upstream, one eye on the little girl, then stepped into the water. The current carried her toward the girl.

A light rain began to fall.

I'm not sure how much time passed. Suddenly, the people around me were in an uproar. The little girl had been saved. The adults pulled her from the water, drenched and exhausted. I watched as the rain drenched me. People were running toward the girl. Joyful voices mixed with sobs. "Are you okay? Open your eyes. Oh, thank God. Thank God you're safe."

The little girl was wearing a red life jacket just like the one Mom had been wearing.

In that instant, I understood what was happening.

Mom wasn't there.

"Mommy… Mommy…!"

I looked around for her.

She was nowhere.

"Mommy…!"

Far away, I heard an ambulance siren. The girl was wrapped in a blanket and carried off by a crowd of adults, leaving the river behind.

Everyone was so caught up in her rescue that they didn't even notice Mom was missing.

"Mommy!!"

I was the only one who kept screaming her name. Over and over and over.

I don't remember very well what happened after that.

When I heard she had been found far downriver, it felt like a lie. Only much later did I notice that the rim of the mug she always used was chipped.

Dad had a picture of Mom framed and placed it in a corner of the kitchen. Every day, he put flowers in the vase beside it.

The neighbors made a point of talking to me whenever they passed me in the street, listening kindly to what I said and offering tearful words of encouragement.

The internet was full of anonymous comments about the accident:

Jumping into a flooded river is basically suicide.

I heard she thought she was a good swimmer, but a river's not a pool.

She died to save someone else's kid. That's not fair to her own kid.

Sucks that we can't hang out by the river anymore because of this.

That's what happens when you try to be a hero.

The people who wrote those things probably don't know what really happened. I bet they forgot what they wrote by the next day. But if you're the one they're writing about, the pain stays with you. Right after the accident, some people I knew showed me the comments, outraged. I was too young to grasp what everything meant. But as I got older and understood more, the unintentional cruelty of those words tormented me. I was still struggling to accept that she was gone. How was I, her next of kin, supposed to deal with all these people acting like the whole thing was her fault, even though she was the one who saved that little girl?

Mom just kept on smiling at me from the photo of her in the kitchen, oblivious to my feelings.

I think the accident caused a crucial shift within me.

One evening, I stood on a chair in Mom's dusty room, wanting to remember our happy times together. I tried singing one of the songs we used to sing.

But once I began, I realized I couldn't sing anymore. It felt like my voice was getting caught in the back of my throat and wouldn't come out of my mouth. I was confused. Something deep in my heart was stopping me from singing.

Why? Why can't I sing?

I started crying.

"Mom," I mumbled. "Mom, why can't I sing anymore?"

I knew the reason singing used to be so fun and feel so necessary was because Mom was listening. But objectively speaking, was it actually such a big deal that I couldn't sing? Nothing bad was going to happen because of it. No one would criticize me for it. Life would go on.

I attended the local middle school. The uniform was suffocating.

A lot of the kids I went to elementary school with commuted to town for middle school. Less than half of us stayed at the local school, so we had combined-grade classes. During chorus practice, the principal accompanied us on piano, and all the students in the school sang together—all thirteen of us. And since there were only thirteen of us, I quickly got caught whenever I mouthed the words instead of singing them. I didn't answer when the teacher asked me why I wasn't singing. I thought I'd get yelled at, but that didn't happen. Instead, I was allowed to sit in a corner of the music room and watch. I must've looked so apathetic just sitting there in silence.

Inside, though, flocks of wordless, bewildering things were swirling through my head. As soon as I got home, I went to Mom's room. Brilliant evening light shone in through the window. The table was piled with cardboard boxes of dishes we didn't use anymore and out-of-season appliances. It had turned into a storeroom. Years had passed since the accident. I wished they hadn't.

I took the records down from the shelves one by one and listened to them. Day after day after day. Listening to them somehow quieted my raging emotions.

But one day, a moment came when I couldn't stand it anymore. As soon as I got home, I went to Mom's room and sat in front of the piano. I opened a notebook and poured all the bewildering things inside me onto the paper. I filled page after page, scribbling furiously.

Why did Mom go into the river and leave me behind? Why did she choose to save some girl she didn't know over her life with me? Why am I all alone? Why, why, why?

I wrote a long, long song, adding pages to the notebook and sticky notes when I ran out of paper. I wrote down the endless melody that welled up inside me. Things that were neither words nor melody, I depicted in pictures. All of them swirled together. It was like an eddy in the river, like a black hole that swallowed everything, like a hole in the top of my head. The floor was covered with pieces of paper scribbled with lyrics and pictures and musical scores.

"……!!"

All of a sudden, I returned to my senses. My pen stopped. I was abruptly aware of how worthless, meaningless, and hideous everything I'd jotted down was.

What am I doing? I thought. I was completely fed up with myself.

I tore the paper into shreds. Without a second thought, I threw everything I had written into an old steel wastepaper basket. The wad of paper looked like fresh vomit.

I somehow made it to high school.

I felt truly worthless. It genuinely felt like my uniform necktie was choking me. I crossed the Chinka Bridge on the way to school staring at my feet.

I'd gotten into a combined junior and senior high school in the city and transferred there once I finished middle school. That was when I met my old friend Shinobu again.

"Suzu?"

"Shinobu..."

He had completely transformed. He was tall and he practically glowed. I, on the other hand, felt like I hadn't grown at all since we last met. Absolutely mortified, I could hardly speak to him. What had I been doing all these years?

Although I was starting a new life commuting to school in the city, I had little interest in studying. I'd passed the test to get in, but in class, I always ended up staring aimlessly out the window. And I knew I shouldn't have, of course.

I didn't join any clubs. Hardly anyone did that.

Before heading home one day, I watched the other kids absorbed in their extracurricular activities. The track club was lined up in the courtyard jumping hurdles. The volleyball team was jogging around the school grounds. The drummers in the brass band were banging their sticks in the hallway, metronomes in their ears. The naginata team was sitting cross-legged on the floor in the training hall, performing their ritual greetings. The freshman baseball players who hadn't gotten their numbers yet were lined up watching intently as the older players practiced.

Feeling out of place, I hurried away from the school.

It was already winter. There's a river called the Kagami that runs through downtown from east to west. Its name means "mirror," and true to form, it's often calm enough to flawlessly reflect the TV tower and office buildings on the far bank.

I was walking along the riverbank on my way to the station when some girls from band skipped past me, laughing, their instruments over their shoulders. The cutesy cat keychains clipped to their schoolbags bounced along as the group forged ahead. Clipped to my bag, I have a cheap plastic keychain of Mr. Reseggnation, a cartoon character shaped like an egg. He has his hand propped against a wall to tolerate the crap he's going through. All that resignation doesn't seem to do much because his head is cracked. Needless to say, there's nothing cutesy about him.

I was in a dark hallway.

"I don't want to!" I said, trying to resist.

But I was pulled into the room all the same. The insulated door slammed shut after me.

"No!"

It was a gaudy karaoke cubicle with pink and purple lights spinning dizzily overhead. I smelled incense. I'd heard there was going to be a party for girls in my class, but as I watched them standing on the sofa, bobbing their heads, I knew I could never fit in with such madness.

"Peggie Sue is so cute!"

"She's super popular on U right now!"

On the wall-mounted monitor, Peggie Sue, a popular AS on U, was singing. She was an eccentric beauty dressed in a black latex dress, with long silver hair, purple lipstick, and red eyes.

Peggie Sue? U? AS? Popular?

I didn't understand any of it. I felt like I lived in a different universe.

"Here."

Suddenly, someone thrust the mic in front of my face, like they were ordering me to sing.

"What?" I blurted out, confused. I hadn't even taken off my coat and scarf.

"Here," another girl said, holding out her mic, too. Why were they doing this to an outsider like me?

"Let's sing something together."

"Yeah, sing!"

They were all forcing their mics on me. What was happening?

"Are you gonna be the only who doesn't sing?"

"The thing about you not being able to sing is a lie, right?"

So that's *what this is about.*

Dozens of mics were right up in my face.

"Uhhh, uhhh…"

I wanted to tell them to stop, that they were hurting me, but no words came out.

"Sing!"

"C'mon, sing for us!"

"Sing something!"

Their voices started sounding like echoes in a cave.

"I told you to sing."

"Sing!"

"Sing!!"

"Arrrgh!" I couldn't help yelling.

The mics clattered to the floor. The girls dancing on the sofa stared at me in shock. There was a bewildered silence.

"What's wrong, Suzu?"

The mics and the girls holding them had vanished like phantoms.

"N-nothing. I'm sorry, I just..."

Without finishing that thought, I pushed the door open with all my might and stumbled into the hallway.

One of the girls must've heard I couldn't sing and told the others.

Snow flurries were falling when I got off the bus, and I almost slipped as I walked down the hill from the bus stop. It snows a lot in Kochi, especially in the mountains. As I crossed the Chinka Bridge, I heard thin ice cracking. The concrete bridge was frozen.

It was so cold.

I didn't fit in, and I didn't like it. I wasn't strong enough to be okay with being alone. I lacked the resolve and the philosophy for that.

I'm not selfish. Is it a lie that I can't sing? Yeah, it's a lie. I've just never had much confidence. I do want to be friends with everyone. I really do. And I know I do. Of course I know...

"Ooh...ooh..."

I stopped in the middle of the bridge and impulsively wrenched out a sound from within me.

"Oooh...oo...oooh..."

I breathed in. The cold air stung my throat. I kept singing to the river anyway.

"Oo...ooh...oooooo...oh..."

I sang?

No, that didn't actually count as a song. More like a groan. My bag slipped off my shoulder. Would people be okay with me if I sang? If I sang, would I be friends with everyone? Singing by myself here wouldn't do any good. I sounded like I was being crushed to death. All the same, I forced my voice to sing the song I used to sing with Mom. I was happy back then. Not now.

The river sucked in the powdery snowflakes. Suddenly, everything went black.

A wave of nausea rose from the pit of my stomach. I pressed my hands over my mouth.

"Urgh…!!"

I crouched down to my knees, unable to hold back the rising stomach acid. I leaned over the edge and vomited into the clear water.

The vomit splattered onto the river's surface, sending out overlapping ripples.

After I threw up everything in my stomach, I stayed collapsed on the bridge.

My hair was all messed up and my mouth was smeared with stinking vomit. *I hate this so much. I just want it all to be over.*

I was trembling and moaning. Stinging tears ran down my cold cheeks. *The world would be better without me.* I listened to the snow gently accumulating around me.

Ping.

My phone had slid out of my bag, and a notification had popped up. It was a message from Hiro.

Suzu, check this out. It's literally incredible lmao, you're gonna love it

There was a link underneath.

U

I went home and opened my MacBook.

Shivering from the cold, I clicked the link from Hiro. The letter "U" floated slowly onto the black screen, accompanied by a pulsating sound.

"...U?"

The screen lit my vomit-spattered face.

An invitation page appeared with a message on it.

U is another reality.
Your AS is another you.
You can't redo life in the real world. But in U, you can.
It's time to live as another you.
It's time to begin a new life.
It's time to change the world.

"......!!"

I stared at the screen, transfixed, forgetting the outside chill.

The app started up automatically on my laptop, syncing with my cell phone lying next to it. The registration page appeared on the screen, asking for my name.

"My name…"

I hesitated. I felt reluctant to enter it. Still, my hands reached out to the keyboard.

S…u…z…

I typed the letters haltingly.

…u

Powerful anxiety welled up inside me. I impulsively tapped the backspace key and closed my MacBook like I was shutting an open door.

"……"

I curled over the table and sighed shakily.

"I wanna be next to Ruka!"

My eyes landed on Ruka, who was sitting on a bench in the courtyard.

Girls were pressed in all around her. Our first year of high school was almost over, so they'd decided to take a group photo.

"I'm sitting next to her!"

"No fair!"

"I wanna be near her!"

Standing in the shadow of a column, I looked longingly at Ruka. I was jealous of the girls who got to take a picture with her.

"Ruka, look over here. I'm gonna take it now," the girl holding the camera said. Ruka looked forward. She must have noticed me then, because she started waving dramatically.

"Hey, Suzu!"

"Me?"

She gestured for me to come over to them.

"Get in the picture with us!"

All the other girls stared at me, obviously wondering what had gotten into her. Panicking, I hid behind the column, then poked my face out and waved dismissively.

"N-no, I'm okay."

She kept gesturing for me to come.

"Hurry up!"

Later, someone sent me the picture. Ruka was surrounded by a group of girls making cute peace signs. My freckle-splattered face was among theirs. I was standing right behind Ruka like some sort of ghost, making the most awkward peace sign.

When I tried registering for U again, I had to upload a photo of myself. I didn't have any. Why would I ever want to take a selfie? So I used that group photo.

A facial recognition marker appeared, asking me to identify myself among the girls. I moved the cursor to the freckled face behind Ruka.

A message appeared. Our AI system is automatically creating a new AS, it read, along with a note: AS is what avatars are called on U. Another you.

Another me.

After a moment, the freshly rendered AS was displayed.

"Huh...?"

The AS was completely different from me, almost frighteningly beautiful. She looked more like Ruka than me.

"Why Ruka...?"

Maybe the AI had gotten us mixed up because we were next to each other in the photo? Pretty sloppy for artificial intelligence. I figured I'd better fix the problem and lifted my finger to hit the BACK button.

"Crap, no. Back, back, cancel..."

Suddenly, I froze. A pattern of red dots was drawn clearly on the AS's face.

"Freckles…"

I instinctively touched my own cheek. Weren't those mine?

"No way… Is that me…?"

I slowly typed one letter at a time into the name field on the registration screen. This time, I didn't write Suzu.

B...e...l...l

The English word for Suzu.

"…Bell."

As soon as I chose a name for the AS, I felt a surge of tenderness for her.

A CANCEL button and an OK button appeared onscreen. I had to choose.

"What should I do…?"

I didn't feel brave enough to claim that beautiful AS was me. I was losing my nerve.

Part of me felt like it didn't matter that she was completely different from the real me. Wasn't the Internet all about distancing yourself from reality? Lots of people used showy names or icons on social media. U was a virtual world, and ASes were virtual people. This world's creators claimed to strictly protect privacy and ensure anonymity. In that case, no one ought to be able to criticize me here.

So why not? I thought. But the next moment, I hesitated.

Why did U's AI system create this beautiful AS for me in the first place? Was it just some chance outcome of indeterminacy? Had it looked deep into my heart and seen my greatest desires? Or…

"Cancel or okay?"

I had to choose.

It was late at night; a desk lamp offered the only light in the study.

Sitting in front of my MacBook, I made up my mind and steadied my breathing.

It's time to live as another you.

The U message looped through my mind.

I clicked the OK button.

The U app on my phone instantly started up, like it had been waiting for this moment.

"Please put on your device," a calm, female voice instructed.

I did as I was told and took a pair of what looked like earbuds out of their case, then popped them into my ears.

"Reading biometric information..."

The U insignia on the device flickered blue. This single device was apparently able to scan all sorts of biological information. Really quickly, too.

"Scan complete," the voice said. Then, as if confirming something, it added, "Now initiating body sharing."

There was a *bwawawawa* sound, like something spinning fast. My head felt like it was wrapped in a rubber band. I'd heard that was caused by the powerful magnetic field that the device generated. Maybe that was why my hair was floating as if I was in an antigravity chamber.

"Syncing vision."

I felt the magnetic field gather at the back of my head.

I slowly opened my eyes.

"Ahhh!!"

Brilliant white light flooded in.

It was cloth. White layers of cloth maybe thirty feet high flapping in the wind. I looked down at my body and my heart skipped a beat.

My feet were floating.

The announcer's voice came again, like a message from heaven.

"Now syncing cognitive functions and deep limb sensations."

What does that mean? I was speechless even in the unreal world, too. Sweat seeped from every pore and my heart pounded in my chest.

"Transferring your sense of bodily autonomy and ownership to your registered AS."

Something approached me slowly from behind. I caught a glimpse of pink hair.

It was the AS I had just registered. But its face was completely blank, like a white plate with nothing on it.

As I stared in a daze, this faceless girl—my embodied AS—was overlayed onto my body. The sensation of a separate body invading my own made my skin crawl. The AS shifted forward and backward like she was adjusting her focus and quickly achieved a perfect fit. Instantly, my disgust vanished.

On the far side of the fluttering white cloth I could see a large white door. I walked slowly toward it, both hands stretched before me.

"Welcome to the world of U," the announcer said.

I put my hands on the door, and it flew open.

As I rushed through the door, a vista of soaring skyscrapers unfolded as far as I could see.

"Whoa…"

Large, bustling avenues crisscrossed in every direction, with crowds of people—no, ASes—floating down them. Some took the form of animals, insects, or ocean creatures, others of vases, triangular rulers, or bicycles, and still others of fantastical half-human beasts, goddesses, or warriors. There were more, too, in every form imaginable, all flying back and forth and talking loudly.

I gazed up at the night sky. At first I thought it was filled with sparkling stars, but then I realized they were the innumerable glimmering windows of upside-down skyscrapers.

Another reality. Another world.

So this is U?

Flurries of snow were falling. It was a little cold. When I reached out my hand to catch a snowflake, I saw a pale arm and long, slender fingers—my own.

"……!"

Surprised by these new physical sensations, I looked down to inspect my body. My slender midriff and long legs were wrapped in a dress so white and unsullied it looked newborn.

And this is me?

A line from thc U welcome message ran through my mind:

It's time to live as another you.

I sensed someone's eyes on me and jerked my head up. Several of the ASes in the crowd were looking at me. But after a quick glance, they walked off. It was like they were saying, *Okay, you might be one of the pretty ones, but this is U. Your looks aren't anything special.*

That was how I liked it. No one gave me a second look. Maybe, then, I could try something I'd been wanting to do for a long time.

I lifted my face, took a deep breath, and sang an experimental note.

My voice was my own, no question about that. It came out far more freely than I'd expected. As a sort of vocal stretch, I kept humming, my nasal cavity vibrating. The sound came out more smoothly than I'd imagined. Was my virtual body improving the sound? But I didn't at all have the sense that the sound was separate from my own consciousness. Was that because my biometric information had been accurately scanned?

Anyway…

"I sang!"

I couldn't believe it. The snow swirled magically around me, my voice echoing between the skyscrapers.

How many years had it been since I really sang? It was strange that despite the gap, and despite my lack of a warm-up, my voice came out exactly as I wanted it to. I felt I'd gotten hold of incredible freedom, but at the same time I was a little scared. How had my biometric information been converted to create this output? What was an AS, really?

Anyway...

"I finally sang!!"

That alone made me irrepressibly happy.

I gathered my concentration and decided to sing a song with proper words. Of course, there was no accompaniment, but I couldn't have cared less.

Gales of song, guide me through the storm

On the wings of a small, simple melody
Words take flight and soar, they carry me
A world will see

Looking for a farewell;
I pull the threads
A life without you I cannot accept
I can't tell that lie
I can't let go

As I sang, ribbons of the lyrics translated into different languages encircled me. Gaelic, Thai, Persian—they were all overlapping and intertwining. Were they generated automatically when the app detected a song? I could also hear synthetic voices singing with me in several languages, though not quite as many.

"Hmm...?"

Maybe that was why the ASes who had ignored me a few minutes earlier were turning back to stare at me.

"Uh...?"

Legions of ASes floating down the roads between the high-rises were stopping one after the next to watch. That wasn't what I had in mind. I'd only wanted to see what the body-sharing technology let me do. And now all these ASes were gathered around listening. I was like a virtual street musician. Mortifying.

But I couldn't stop partway through the song. I wanted to sing it to the end, for myself. So I kept going.

But now that you're gone,
I have to move on
Seems like everyone,
Just smile staring at the sun
But what about me?
Tell me how I will know
where I should go?
Oh gales, you sing and guide me!

I walk alone
There's more to life I have to know
It's just me, lost and so far away from home,
alone I
shut myself in
Still the winds howl, they call and their voices lead me,

Gales of song, guide me through the storm
Let the melody lift me high, I'll be me

Gales of song, please stay by my side
Winds of love, breathe into my life

Comment bubbles from the ASes who'd been listening started popping up:

What's going on?

Who's singing?

Strange song

At first, the comments were cautious, like people were waiting to see what would happen. Soon, though, their hesitation vanished.

Wish she'd shut up.

That song's weird.

What a poser

For some reason, the ASes writing that stuff were all so cute, you'd never expect them to say things like that. They had on frilly pink dresses or were small animals or babies clutching teddy bears.

She's not bad looking

What's with the freckles? LOL

As I sang, all different comments flew at me. I ignored them. I was singing for myself. I couldn't help feeling hurt, though. I noticed that they were coming from a certain small group of viewers. It was hard. Maybe that was written all over my face. The attacks escalated.

Freak

Stop already!

Shut up!

Somehow, I finished the song without giving up. The ASes who'd been making all the fuss sighed, snorted, and left. I watched them go, feeling depressed.

Then I heard someone call my name.

"Bell?"

I looked up.

"Oh!"

A strange creature was gliding toward me.

"What…? Oh!"

Shedding shiny scales, it circled beneath me, then alighted softly on my hand. It was a very odd AS, like a white fairy, or an angel—a sea angel. I looked closer. Its body was translucent, like a delicate piece of *warabimochi*. It fluttered its wings and said, in a slightly faltering voice, "You…are amazing. You…are beautiful."

I felt I'd been rescued.

"…Hee-hee. Thank you."

I opened my eyes. It was morning.

Somehow, I'd ended up facedown on my bed.

Was everything a dream? It felt too vivid for that. I looked at my phone to figure out the answer.

There was the profile page I'd made for Bell. It wasn't a dream.

I looked at the icon below her name, where the number of followers was posted.

Bell: 0 followers

Zero.

"No followers," I mumbled, staring at the screen. "Different world, same story."

Even though I hadn't set out to rack up followers, I felt kind of disappointed.

Just then, I got a notification. My follower number changed to 1. It was the angel AS. A comment bubble appeared; it was blank.

I put my phone down and lay on my back on my bed, thinking about what happened the night before. Lots of it had been unexpected.

"And I was finally able to sing..."

That hit me harder than anything else. The winter morning light felt more brilliant than usual. I hadn't felt that fresh and new in ages.

Another follower notification pinged. It was Hiro. Her AS was a cute bird with a round hat. The subject line of her message was Re: Just saw you. It read:

It's Hiro. You're awesome, Suzu (Bell). I got you, girl!

FLUX

Signing up on U didn't really change much. I didn't get many followers. Every couple of days, I'd get a new follower notification, but I never checked who it was. Nothing annoying happened for a while, and I was enjoying the uneventful days. I felt so contented, I didn't have time to worry about the virtual world.

Spring came.

In the mornings, I crossed the Chinka Bridge. I didn't look down like I used to. Instead I faced forward, striding over the bridge with Mr. Reseggnation bouncing against my school bag. My feet felt light, like I could skip along the road at any moment. I felt indescribably free. I was surprised by how dramatically the simple act of singing in U had changed my mood.

I finally felt like a normal high school student.

I started my junior year. I looked at the blackboard like a good student and felt hopeful about my classes. At lunch, I met up with Hiro and went to the school commissary. I picked over the array of stuffed breads at the bakery counter, which was always packed. We'd go back to the classroom, and while we ate, Hiro would spout off reviews of the latest books she was reading. She talked about the crucial turning points in human history and the contradiction between freedom and equality and the imbalance between scientific development and the human spirit and so on and so forth.

After school, I wandered along by myself, listening to my favorite bands' new songs with my earbuds in. I bought ice cream at the sweet shop I'd always been curious about. I squatted down to pet the white cat stretched out in the sun in front of the church. I walked along the road by the river, looking up at the evening sky.

At night, I took long, relaxing baths. I dried my hair, put on pajamas, reorganized my notes from class, and got ready for the next day.

The days passed without much happening.

The next thing I knew, it was the start of summer. In gym class, we ran around the track as the blinding sun reflected off it into our eyes. Everyone dragged their feet, complaining about how hot it was or how they felt like throwing up. Secretly, I was having a great time. I used to hate gym class, but not anymore. I felt light, like I could run forever.

I went back to class pleasantly sweaty and changed into my uniform. Classes were over for the day. I thought about where to stop on the way home from school.

A refreshing breeze ruffled the curtains. I tightened my necktie, stuffed my gym clothes into my bag, and checked my phone. There was a follower notification. I opened the U app absentmindedly.

Bell: 32,460,428 followers

"What the...?"

What's happening?

I had more than thirty million followers. As I watched, the number rose with dizzying speed.

Why?

A video of the song Bell had sung a cappella on that snowy night had been shared around the world. Not only that, but the video had loads of "related videos" linked to it.

"What related videos...?"

Sounds had been added to Bell's simple a cappella song and chords layered on, transforming it into a standard pop number. *Who did that?* No sooner had that question crossed my mind than I discovered that someone had used a vocoder to turn Bell's voice robotic. Before I could register shock, the song morphed into a classy jazz band accompaniment, which slid into a red-blooded heavy rock version.

What the heck?

As I stared at the screen, remakes in all imaginable genres flashed past. Hip-hop, string quartet, reggae, folk, bossa nova, EDM... Bell's song had been adapted into all these genres by the most skilled of musicians. They melded together into a single grand collaboration. It was like a magnificent operatic suite played by an orchestra.

That wasn't all.

Bell had been wearing a simple white dress, but now versions of her dressed in all different outfits proliferated everywhere. With each outfit, she made a dizzyingly different impression. She was a pop idol, an opera singer, a nineties-era grunge singer, an athlete, a flapper, or dressed in menswear or an exosuit. Then she was a cybergoth, a biker babe, a coverall-clad worker, a gangster, a bicycle racer, a UFC fighter, a cyberpunk, a modern geisha, a baseball player... The list was endless.

Millions of ASes were commenting from around the world:

What the heck, this is awesome

I've never heard anything like this.

This arrangement's wild

Damn she can sing

She's got a quirky kind of beauty.

What's this song called?

I searched but I can't find it!

Her fashion sense is crazy

I'm obsessed with her

Someone tell me who Bell is!

The more comment bubbles appeared, the higher the follower number climbed.

Bell: 38,641,027 followers

Bell was going viral.

Then the popular singer Peggie Sue interrupted.

"Bell? Yeah, I've heard some of her music, but she's nothing special, y'know?"

She was draped over an expensive-looking sofa and wore a haughty expression, like she was talking down to some underlings.

ASes critical of Bell started liking Peggie Sue's interview, and it suddenly generated a buzz.

She's right!

Her voice is so grating.

Bell's a huge diva

Is she betting on her sex appeal?

Trashy.

Classic online bashing. The bubbles popped up one after another, igniting a fire.

She doesn't know the basics of songwriting.

It's only good because of the arrangements

Her outfit doesn't go with the song

The lyrics are way too personal

Bell had only just arrived in U, but the critical ASes were already slamming her.

Don't tell me she's trying to be some artiste

She lets other people do all the work.

Scathing bubbles filled the screen until I couldn't even see Bell's video.

Take music seriously, dammit!

The critics were all screaming in unison. But that, too, turned out to only be a tiny blip. U was way bigger than they thought.

Still...

I'm just really into this song for some reason

Why?

How come?

In order to ensure a fair range of views unswayed by fake news, hate, prejudice, or extremism, U used a powerful verification system that other social media platforms didn't have. As if to prove that system's effectiveness, the initial critical response to Bell shifted over time to an increasingly positive one.

I feel like she's singing for me.

It's like a private concert just for me.

No, she's singing for me!

No, for me!

Why?

How come?

Tell me!

All these comments and images and videos related to Bell came together like the parts of a mosaic, forming multiple windows onto a single enormous picture.

That picture *was* Bell, or at least the general image of her created by the combined consciousnesses of everyone on U.

On her back was a pair of huge, outstretched white wings.

She was like a glimmering angel fluttering down to U.

* * *

"......!!"

I stood there blinking wide-eyed at this incredible development. How could she have more than thirty-eight *million* followers? My face was twitching.

"Hey, have you heard of Bell?" I heard someone say. I glanced back at the classroom in surprise. Some girls were talking as they changed out of their gym clothes.

"Of course I have!"

"Who's Bell?"

"You mean that girl on U?"

"She's pretty amazing."

Seriously? The ripples were spreading into the real world. My heart was pounding in my ears. I didn't know what to do.

I hunched over and tried to sneak out of the classroom. I must have looked suspicious, because one of the girls called out to me as she pulled up her socks.

"Suzu?"

I darted from the room, down the hall, and out of the school before hurrying through the shopping arcade in Obiyamachi.

This was serious.

Very serious.

Hiro, I'm in trouble!

I broke into a frantic run. I couldn't process this on my own. I was headed for Hiro's house, but I was so worked up I accidentally ran past the front door. I backed up and dove into the entryway.

"Hello!" I spluttered.

Hiro's mother came out to greet me in a summery lace top. "Oh, hi, Suzu! Hiroka's in the sitting room."

Hiro's family owns the local bank. They live in an old-fashioned mansion downtown, with who knows how many rooms in it. I clattered down the long, wood-floored hallway and burst into one of the sitting rooms.

"Hiro! You won't believe what happened!! Bell—"

Hiro had turned the teahouse-style sitting room into her study. Several large monitors loomed over a computer set up on a low table, and piles of thick, hard-cover tomes and art books crowded every available space.

"I know," she said, spinning to face me in her leather chair like a queen. "She's on U's Global Music Hits chart. As I expected."

"No, not that! People are trash-talking her like crazy!!" I shrieked, standing in front of a Kawada Shoryo partition screen. Hiro remained unruffled as she glanced at the social media feed on one of her monitors.

"I expected that, too," she said. "People are just freaked out because she's so good. Hmph. If you only get positive comments, it means you just have intense fans. That's the minor leagues. On U, it's the honest feedback from both sides that polishes true talent."

I gripped my head and writhed in agony.

"So half of them hate her?! I'm gonna die! I'm legit gonna die!!"

"That means the other half love her. Have some confidence!" she snapped. "Why do you think they like her?"

"...Because she looks like Ruka."

"And?"

"Because some people arrange her songs."

"And?"

"Because you're the producer. Plus the clothes and dance moves and—"

"No!! I mean yes, but no!!" Hiro banged on the monitor. "The biggest reason is because this is U! U's body-sharing technology draws out each user's hidden abilities. If it didn't, you'd be spending the rest of your life crying like a little baby instead of singing. Oh, and look at this."

She shoved her phone in my face. The message on the screen read Who is Bell?

"Bell's true identity… Eek! Why are they trying to figure out who she is?!"

"They're so off the mark it's hilarious. Do they honestly think she's some big-name celebrity?" Hiro cackled demonically.

"This isn't funny at all!"

"No one would ever guess Bell's actually a frumpy teenager from the sticks," she said, cackling again.

"You're scary," I said, hugging myself.

"This is the funnest game ever. I'm gonna turn this gloomy freckle-faced high school girl into a U megastar. Heh-heh-heh!"

On screen, top designers were dressing Bell in various outfits. Hiro's AS with the little round hat pointed at the scene in sync with the real Hiro's motions. When Hiro's shoulders shook with laughter, her AS's shoulders shook, too.

"You might make tons of money, but don't worry. I'll donate all of it anonymously to charities for you."

Another window on the screen was cluttered with articles about child abuse, child poverty, and similar topics. She probably did intend to give all the money away.

My eyes rested on an article about single fathers. There was a picture of a kindly-looking dad and his two sons, both of whom looked younger than me. I wasn't the only kid in the world with a single parent. Was Hiro planning to give them some money if Bell became a success?

* * *

Bell was standing on the whale's head, belting out a song.

lalalai
lalalai

How can I
find a love lost in time? There's an answer in the stars for me
All the way across the galaxy; go on forever

lalalai
lalalai
I will follow the signs
'cause I know when I reach the end it's you I'll see
But we can't waste the time here, it's now or never

The relentless force of nature
The visage of our future
Sometimes I know it feels like fate is never on our side
But as I stand inside the vortex
I wanna have you here beside me
It's all I need to leap into a perfect sky!

Stand up, the party's over here
Come one, come all, jump into the fire

Keep up, let go of your fears
Stand proud and tall, we will never grow tired

Line up; the party's right here
Come one, come all, let's follow the north star

Step in, you are whatever you wanna be,
you are free, just like all of us are

Dance away a world you never loved from the start
It's our ride to the future, are you ready to depart?

"It's Bell!"

"Bell!!"

The ASes gazed up at her, screaming her name.

Bell is our new diva.

Don't you think she should spell her name Belle?

Belle?

It means beautiful in French

It's perfect for her, because she's not perfect.

It's an amazing name, to put it mildly!

The cheers of millions of ASes echoed between the skyscrapers.

"Belle!"

"Belle!!"

"Belle!"

"Belle!!"

"Belle!!"

Belle crossed her arms over her chest and flung them open. Graphical images of flowers burst from her body, drifting down on the city from above the placid floating whale. She belted out her song as if she was blessing all people, all things, all life.

Faced with a presence this strong, the power of the critical speech bubbles wilted. They sounded like mere jealousy and resentment.

As a professional music critic, I say two thumbs down.

She's so fake

Overproduced and sloppy

I don't get why everyone loves her

On her private channel, Peggie Sue flipped her hair and ranted.

"You've gotta be kidding! She's outranking me?! Get serious!"

But her window was soon crowded with biting comments:

Oh, it's Peggie Sue.

So yesterday.

idk her

She's still around?

What a hag.

She went pale and tried beating back the proliferating bubbles.

"What the? Hey! I'm drowning! Stop! Gahhh!!"

But her resistance was in vain. In seconds, her window was obliterated by bubbles.

"Stay jealous, you ignorant saps!" Hiro's AS screamed victoriously, laughing so hard you could see her tonsils. "Belle changed the world!! Give it up for Belle! Go, go, go!! Belle is awesoooome!!"

The real Hiro was cackling uncontrollably in front of her computer monitor.

"Hiroka, what are you laughing about?!" her father interrupted furiously, his arms crossed as he towered behind her. Her mother was standing next to him, looking upset.

"He told me you can't use this room anymore," she said defeatedly.

* * *

The boisterous voices of the women's choir echoed through the school building.

I graduated from this elementary school, but it's not used anymore. The weedy playground has been turned into a parking lot; it's now full of cars. The shelves where we used to leave our shoes are empty. In the hallway, long meeting tables are stacked on top of each other, and maps of the Niyodo River drawn by kids are peeling from the wall. The desks are gone from the classrooms, replaced by a jumble of triangular rulers, computer monitors, disaster-response helmets, and other junk.

The word "Graduation" was still written on a blackboard, as if time had stopped. The gym had become a storage vault full of discarded instruments, folding chairs, and benches. A wooden plaque carved with the faces of graduates hung on the wall. In the 1990s, there were several in each class, but by the early 2010s, there were only two or three students graduating each year. Then there were a few years with just one student (me), and that was where the carvings ended.

Five women were standing on the stage in the gym, singing.

"Alle psallite cum luya." We sing and play our lyres.

Alle psallite cum luya
Alle concrepando psallite cum luya
Alle corde voto Deo toto, psallite cum luya
Alleluya

This choral group was made up of five feisty women in their forties through their seventies, all with various backgrounds and careers. They called themselves the Choir Squad. The gym's rafters echoed with their voices like it was a church.

When they finished their hymn, they caught their breath and

began examining their sheet music. Today's practice was being observed by a group of visitors from some other town, who began to clap hesitantly.

The local government employee who was leading their tour said awkwardly, "As you can see, we've been working to find creative community uses for our old school buildings. Now if you'll just follow me..."

With that, he herded the visitors toward the exit. Ms. Kita, who was wearing a tie-dyed dress, fanned her face as if to pull herself together.

"It's hard to get excited about practicing Christmas songs with all the cicadas making such a racket," she said.

That made their schedule sound easygoing, but the fact was, they had just finished a summer concert and had music festivals or senior center performances lined up nearly every month. They all had full-time jobs, too. Ms. Kita was talking about their next major concert at the end of the year.

Mom used to belong to this choir. After she died, I joined in her place. Or to put it more honestly, they felt bad for me and invited me to join them whenever they practiced. I would hide behind a column and watch them, secretly singing along under my breath. That was the sort of "member" I'd been since I was little. Today, as usual, I had burrowed under the marimba and was whispering along to their songs.

"Suzu! Come out here and sing!" commanded Ms. Nakai, leaning over in her orange sleeveless shirt to look me in the face. I got onto my knees and crawled away.

"Nope, nope, nope."

"Choir members don't hide in the shadows. What are you, a bell cricket?"

"I am, and I'm perfectly fine with that," I said, sticking my head between the legs of the keyboard.

"The youngest member ought to be front and center," said Ms. Hatanaka, a scarf around her neck.

"No thank you."

Ms. Yoshitani, with the cute white bob, crossed her arms and sighed. "What to do? Kids these days have no drive."

"It's like she's given up on being happy," said Ms. Kita.

Ms. Okumoto, in her denim jacket and ponytail, put her hand on her hip, as usual. "I'm sure your mother wants you to be happy."

"But how?" I asked them. "How do I achieve happiness?"

They were flummoxed.

"Well, if you put it like that...," said Ms. Okumoto, glancing around pensively.

"H-happiness...," said Ms. Hatanaka, at a loss for words as she frowned behind her glasses.

"Happiness...," Ms. Kita echoed, looking up at the ceiling.

"Happi...ness...," said Ms. Nakai with an awkward gesture that I suppose was meant to embody happiness.

Each of them had lived a unique life. One lived with her long-time partner, another was focused on her career and had never married, another was a twice-divorced single mother, and another cared for her ill husband while raising their children.

Ms. Yoshitani, the oldest, looked around at the other four.

"Funnily enough, I still don't know what it means to be happy even at my age," she said with a laugh, her hand on her chest. The other four stiffened, as if they'd suddenly realized none of them had the right to lecture me on happiness. I peered out from between the legs of the keyboard and looked at each woman in turn.

"…What are you looking at?!" Ms. Kita howled angrily. "You're comparing us, aren't you?"

"I bet you're trying to figure out which of us is right!" said Ms. Hatanaka, her eyes crackling behind her glasses.

"We wouldn't be struggling like this if there was a right way to achieve happiness!" Ms. Nakai shouted.

Terrifying.

I shrank into the shadows beneath the keyboard.

The truth was, I was struggling myself.

I looked down from the breezeway at the basketball court where Shinobu had been playing the other day. No one was around. The ball lay forlornly on the court.

As I stared at it, an indelible memory flashed across my mind.

It was evening. My six-year-old self was squatting down, crying, but everyone kept their distance. Shinobu came up to me holding a mini basketball.

"*Why are you crying?*" he asked, standing by my side.

I just kept sobbing.

"*Why won't you say anything?*" he asked.

I didn't respond.

I can bring this memory up whenever I want. It means a lot to me. I don't know how many times I've replayed it in my mind. I'll probably keep recalling it now and then to make sure I don't forget it. Even when I'm an adult, even when I'm an old woman like Ms. Yoshitani. Forever…

I didn't notice that someone had walked over to me.

"…Suzu?"

I looked up in surprise.

"...Sh-Shinobu?!"

I panicked. What expression had I been making? Cold sweat broke out all over me. I didn't want him to see me looking weird.

"How's your dad?"

"Fine, I guess."

"You guess? Have you been eating okay?"

"I'm e-eating."

I couldn't stand it anymore. I made a move to leave, but he grabbed my hand.

I stared up at him in shock, my face flushing at his touch.

"Did something happen?" he asked me calmly.

"...No."

I glanced down. I didn't want him to see me like this.

"I don't believe you."

"I told you it's fine."

I averted my gaze.

"Look at me," he said.

"...I can't."

"Come on."

Why is he being so pushy? I hesitated, but eventually gave in and looked at him.

He gazed straight into my eyes.

"Talk to me."

"......!!"

His eyes were boring right into mine. My breath caught in my throat. I felt pinned to the spot, transfixed by him.

He'd looked at me the same way on that day when we were kids. He'd squatted down next to me and said, "Talk to me." His eyes hadn't changed a bit. I was in a daze, unable to say a word.

I suddenly felt other eyes on me. A group of girls had noticed us and were whispering to each other.

Dammit.

I let go of Shinobu's hand and hurried away.

"...Suzu!" he called after me, but I kept my gaze fixed ahead as I rounded the hallway corner.

I had to tell him.

I pressed my back against the wall, my hand throbbing where he'd touched it, and practiced what I was going to say.

"Shinobu, I'm not like I was in elementary school. You don't have to keep worrying about me forever..."

Once I got my wits about me, I retraced my steps. I could see him on the far side of the breezeway. I had to tell him. But suddenly, I stopped in my tracks.

"......!"

Ruka was standing in front of him.

She was pointing at a page in her textbook or something and smiling happily at him. She had the kind of radiant beauty that no one could tarnish. Her smile was so perfect, it seemed like the whole world had blessed her. Two other girls were watching from behind, also smiling. They'd been whispering before, but now they looked relieved. I thought I knew why.

I swallowed what I'd planned to say to Shinobu and stored the words deep in my heart. Then I walked away like nothing had happened.

AN ENCOUNTER

The shining moon slid over the equator, bringing twilight to the world of U.

The streets of U, twisting and winding like a huge river, were more crowded than usual today. A curious excitement hovered in the air; everyone seemed restless. Countless online news stories were being broadcast in different languages.

"…In just a few moments, at 20:25 U Standard Time, Belle will take the stage in Spherical Stadium for her largest concert yet," one of the announcers said.

U's city was made up mostly of two kinds of modules—skyscrapers and parks—but lots of other modules existed, too. One was the Spherical Stadium module.

"As many as one or two hundred million ASes around the world are said to be watching, a record for a new talent in the past six months," the announcer continued.

From up close, it was clear that the stadium was formed from many clusters of smaller units. Spectators entered the sphere through the gaps between the units, each of which had multiple windows. The windows were shaped like smartphone screens, with Ases inside them. These were the stadium seats.

The multitudes of ASes were waiting eagerly for the show to begin.

At last, the start time arrived.

With a loud rumble, the sphere's yawning interior gradually darkened. The units drew together, narrowing the gaps between them. Finally, there came a deafening roar; the gaps closed entirely, plunging the inside into blackness. A red line like the equator hovered in the dark.

The concert was beginning.

Music began to play.

An enormous teardrop hovered in the center of the sphere. The spectators watched this strange scene with bated breath, curious to see what would happen. The surface of the drop quivered with tension as something inside began emitting light. A constellation of lights accumulated inside the drop.

Finally, the glowing teardrop exploded like the Big Bang.

Behind the eruption of water, a mysterious, shining form appeared.

It was an enormous dress, thirty feet tall or more, woven from delicate beads.

Emerging from the very top of the dress was Belle—that is, me.

"Wowww…!!"

The cheers of ASes rumbled like an earthquake. A mosaic of light shone from the countless windows of the audience seats. The beads of my dress changed color as they caught the light. They were special light-sensitive beads. It was an incredible costume; everything from the headpiece to the high heels had been made by top designers.

I floated in midair, shifting colors as the light refracted off me. Parts of the dress began to break off like a multistage rocket: first the big parts, then the tiny beads, one by one. The beads started swirling like a whirlpool, transforming into the undulations of a virtual ocean.

Three baby whales wearing headphones appeared and floated

slowly toward me. These whales were top-class dancers who we'd hired for the concert. One of them beat the ocean's surface in time to the music with her tail, sending out beautiful ripples. Another did the same, the ripples intersecting. The third baby whale sent a powerful spray of water out through her blowhole.

Then it was my turn.

I surrendered myself to the rhythm like the whales had, twisting my body and beating the surface of the water. Beautiful ripples flowed outward. I twisted and beat the water again, the ripples overlapping. Then I soared upward, like I was the water spouting from the whale's blowhole.

The whales joined in again and began a coordinated dance around me.

I started to sing.

The flashes of cameras in the audience reached my dress, changing the color of its beads kaleidoscopically. It was inexpressibly beautiful.

The colors were a collaboration of me and the designers and the audience, without whose phone cameras this spectacle would not have existed. I think it felt so special because unlike most things in the digital world, where reproduction is the norm, it could never be re-created.

I belted out the last notes of my song.

"Ooooooooooooh…!!"

Thunderous cheers shook the stadium.

The flashes faded, leaving only the red line in the darkness. The intro to the second song began. The next set, a graphical projection of a steel frame, slid toward me from above and below. During the blackout, Hiro's AS—who had produced the whole show—came skidding toward me.

"Incredible performance, Belle. Ready for the next song?"

"Yeah."

Hiro's AS tossed me the scrap of cloth she'd been holding. It fluttered around me, transforming into a patchwork dress. It was designed by the same person who concocted the bead dress using light-reactive fiber.

Suddenly, I heard a strange *bang*.

"Oh…"

The gaps in the stadium opened ever so slightly.

"Who's opening the doors without permission?!" Hiro's AS screamed.

A group of figures slipped through the tiny crack between the units. One was in the lead, followed by a pack of ASes. They squeezed between the units, almost scraping the walls. The spectators were clearly upset.

"Get out, assholes!" Hiro shrieked with redoubled fury.

The AS in the lead seemed to be running from the group behind it.

"Is it being chased?" I asked.

The group followed the arch of the sphere's equator. The pursuers split into two groups.

"What the hell is that?!" Hiro asked, craning her neck up.

Comment bubbles from U's global hive mind popped up instantly:

Lóng

dragón

龍

naga

Dragon

اژدها

Dreki

Ejderha

"A dragon?"

A hideous monster AS that lives in U.

The creature had two horns, a long snout, and sharp fangs and claws. It looked just like a stereotypical dragon, and it appeared quite violent. But its crimson cloak with a standing collar and the white frills protruding from the cuffs of its suit brought to mind some sort of young nobleman. These two extremes existed in a strange balance. The gaze I glimpsed between locks of its long, curly hair struck me as deeply mysterious.

The pursuers were all dressed in white battle suits lined with red. They looked like the very picture of righteous heroes.

The Dragon rushed upward, his cloak flying, then twisted midair and plunged down. The tricky maneuver shook off his pursuers, but now the second group, who had split off a moment earlier, flew toward him.

The AS in the lead, who was wearing a stone mask, hurtled forward fearlessly.

The opponents crashed head-on into each other, and a shower of crackling sparks erupted.

The Dragon delivered a series of punches so swift I could hardly follow them with my eyes. The pursuers recoiled like so many scattered pebbles. Light like ice crystals shot from them, and they went still. The force of the blows had destroyed their data, freezing them.

I stared at the Dragon in a daze.

"Amazing," I said.

"Who is that?" Hiro's AS asked. Comment bubbles answered right away:

Showed up out of nowhere at U's martial arts hall a few months ago

He's been breaking the record for most consecutive wins

He fights dirty tho

"What do you mean?"

The Dragon landed on a wall unit and switched directions, attacking the group of pursuers he'd shaken off earlier. Without giving them a chance to escape, he knocked them out, one after the next. Crystal images appeared, meaning they were frozen.

He ruins the matches.

He attacks until his opponent's data gets corrupted

It's like he's trying to vent his anger

I stared at the Dragon, dumbfounded.

"Oh!" I gasped, noticing the patterns all over his tattered back. "What are those...?"

He's showing off his bruises, so obnoxious

I looked more closely.

"He has that many...?"

The band of pursuers had swelled. Their leader with the locs gestured, and a dozen or so headed forward, shouting in unison.

Although the Dragon had no one on his side, he turned instantly in their direction, slicing his hands through the air with dazzling speed. The pursuers flew backward.

"Ahhhhh!"

Every last one of them collapsed in a heap. Their leader stared in shock at the decimated troops, then let out a bizarre howl and flew chaotically at the Dragon.

A second later, the Dragon's powerful fist slammed into his face, followed by an uppercut. The AS with the locs was sent flying, their body arched backward from the impact.

"Who's chasing him?" Hiro's AS asked curiously.

The Justices.

"Justices?"

They claim they're the keepers of justice and order in U.

A group of ASes were looking down on the fight from a distance. Like the one with the stone mask and the one with locs, they were leaders of the Justice Corps. They looked strong, like you'd imagine defenders of justice to look. Half of them were female.

"Huh. They look like superheroes," said Hiro's AS, eyeing them over.

A large group of Justices brandishing lances, hammers, Chinese broadswords, and all kinds of other weapons were encircling the Dragon. With a roar, they attacked.

It was one against many. The Dragon seemed to have no chance of winning.

He slowly crossed his arms. Then, with terrific speed, he ripped through the air and sliced into the Justices as if he really were wielding a sword. The tight knot of opponents surrounding him hurtled away all at once.

"Ahhhhh!!"

They were shooting crystal-shaped beams of light.

Every spectator in the stadium was watching, spellbound.

The Dragon turned away and rose slowly on his hind legs. The leaders of the Justices muttered among themselves in astonishment.

"How awful…!"

"Why's he have to take it that far?!"

"Does he want to make this all about himself?!"

They went on like that, criticizing the Dragon righteously. This set off booing from some of the spectators.

"They're right!"

"That asshole ruined Belle's concert!"

"How do we make him pay for this?!"

Soon the cries spread through the whole stadium.

"Apologize to Belle!"

"Quit wasting our time!"

"Get out of here!"

"Get out!"

A weird mood engulfed the stadium. I looked around. Almost every AS present had turned on this lone opponent and was booing him thunderously.

The Dragon stood alone in the center of it all. To me, the bruises covering his back seemed almost like a physical manifestation of all the criticism he was enduring.

Without thinking, I spoke to him.

"Who…"

He turned slowly toward me and took me in with his sharp eyes, but said nothing.

"…are you?"

I asked the words that came to my mind.

Finally, he opened his mouth. His voice was garbled, like he was speaking through a filter.

"…Don't look."

"What…?"

"Don't look at me."

The eyes staring at me from between the mess of curls held rejection. I could ask no more.

Just then, a sharp voice echoed across the stadium.

"Beast!!"

A man confronted the Dragon imposingly.

"I won't allow this. I will not stand for it! As long as this dragon lives, U will have no peace!!" he thundered, arms crossed.

"Is that their leader?" Hiro's AS asked.

Yeah. His name is Justin.

He had bristly blond hair and blue eyes. His imposing, muscular body brought to mind strength and bravery, while his white battle-suit evoked a noble character. He was the very image of a hero, a great man, an ally of justice, a savior.

Justin raised his right arm and pointed to the insignia on his wrist.

"See this?!"

The insignia glowed and swelled, metamorphosing into a metal winged lion's head. From the lion's mouth, a bolt-action mechanism discharged a jewel-like lens. It looked like a cannon.

Justin held it up for all to see.

"Behold the light of truth that safeguards justice and order in U! We shall unveil the evil Beast!!" he proclaimed in a voice so loud it could probably be heard in every corner of U. Banners printed with the names of corporations unfurled behind him in rapid succession. Apparently, these were his sponsors.

Hiro's AS pointed at them, wide-eyed.

"Look at all those sponsor logos!"

"What's he mean by *umbale*?" I asked.

"Unveil," she answered, making a peek-a-boo gesture.

Justin positioned his right arm as if he was taking aim. The inside of the cannon glowed with a mosaic of colors. The particles of color converged, emitting a green light.

Pwaaa!

The light ripped through the darkness, straight toward the Dragon.

He dodged by a hair.

Again, the particles of light converged in Justin's right hand. He fired a second shot.

The agile Dragon evaded, keeping his distance. He seemed quite wary of this mysterious light.

"Rrgh...," Justin snarled, lowering his arm. His moving target was apparently too far away for the long, slender beam of light.

"The doors!!" he commanded, signaling to his troops.

They scattered in all directions. A moment later, the units began rumbling as the gaps between them narrowed.

"Oh no…" I gasped.

The light faded. Once the units slammed shut, darkness engulfed the stadium.

Several searchlights operated by the leaders of the Justices switched on in unison and lit up the Dragon where they converged.

"It's over, Beast!! We will rip the veil from your hideous origin here and now!"

A cry rose from the crowd.

"Oooooooooh!"

They were all on Justin's side.

"Yeah! Do it, do it!!" Hiro's AS piled on.

Rip the veil from his origin? They can do that?

A moment ago, Justin had promised to "unveil the evil Beast" with the "light of justice and order that safeguards U"—that green light. He must've meant that he intended to reveal the identity of the person manipulating the Dragon in the real world. In other words, he was going to violate the privacy that U's security was supposed to guarantee for all members. That was how I interpreted the word "unveil."

I doubted anyone would protest if the AS being unveiled was someone so universally despised. But what if the shoe were on the other foot? No one would want to be unveiled themself. Wasn't it supposed to be forbidden? Wasn't everyone supposed to be equally protected?

The leaders advanced toward the Dragon, searchlights in hand.

The Dragon blocked his eyes with his hands, as if he hated the blinding blur of light. The leaders kept their lights trained mercilessly on him. He seemed frozen by the brilliance.

From a distance, Justin carefully took aim.

The lights drew closer on each side. Keeping them fixed on the motionless Dragon seemed to me unbearably cruel.

The inside of the cannon gleamed, the beams merging.

"Get him!" Hiro's AS screamed excitedly.

I stared silently at the Dragon.

Perhaps he noticed me, because he looked up in my direction. Our eyes met. My heart pounded.

"Wha?!"

Suddenly, the Dragon bounded toward me. The searchlights wavered uncertainly, their target abruptly gone.

"Hmph."

Justin lowered the gun, then quickly raised it again and fired two shots in rapid succession.

But the Dragon slipped past the light beams and hurtled straight at me.

"Ahhhhhh!!" Hiro's AS and I screamed. We were too overwhelmed to move.

The Dragon bore down on us with ferocious speed.

He's gonna hit us!

"Eek!" I screamed again.

But the Dragon merely skimmed past. A blast of wind followed a second later. The Dragon kept climbing, then twisted in midair to land on the set's steel structure. Hiro's AS looked up at him, enraged.

"Watch it, asshole!! You could've hurt Belle!!"

Wrenching loose one of the steel bars, the Dragon dove toward us again.

"No!!"

Again, he skimmed past us at high speed as we hunched in fear. He was aiming for Justin and the other leaders.

"Whoaaaa!!"

They screamed and scattered, dropping their searchlights. The Dragon followed in hot pursuit, brandishing the metal bar over his head as if to say he didn't intend to let them escape.

The searchlights flickered off, plunging the stadium into darkness once again.

I heard a brutal impact, followed by the pained howls of the leaders. What was happening in the darkness? An invisible terror held the audience in thrall.

"Open...open the doors!!" Justin screamed, as if he could hold out no longer.

Gaps in the stadium walls cracked open, practically at his command. The heart-rending forms of the fallen, motionless leaders were bathed in light.

I wondered how many ASes the Dragon had managed to freeze in that short time. His power was overwhelming.

Justin backed away, his face stiff.

"I...I will not tolerate this...!"

The Dragon tossed aside the metal bar and soared off in the opposite direction. I followed him with my eyes.

"I'll unveil him if it's the last thing I do!" Justin screamed, swearing his revenge.

The Dragon acted like he didn't hear his enemy's words, flying between a gap in the stadium roof before vanishing.

For the longest time, I kept staring at the empty space where he had been.

"Who...are you...?"

A SEARCH

Every morning, I take Fugue for a walk. We go down the hill from my house and along the banks of the Niyodo. When I look back from the other side of the Chinka Bridge, my little village glows in the morning light. I see it all the time, but every day its beauty is a little different. Sometimes there are new green leaves, sometimes red and orange ones. The river's water level, the position of the clouds, the drift of the mist, whether any sunbeams are visible, whether it's hot and humid or cold—all these things have endless variations. Their beauty captivates me.

One day on our morning walk, I snapped out of my reverie to see Fugue staring at me like he wanted to play. He doesn't seem to mind that his right paw is missing; he runs and jumps and splashes in the water like any other dog. Seeing that makes me feel kind of relieved, in a way.

When we got back to the house, I took off his leash and fed him. Then I paused on the porch to wipe his feet before we both went inside.

"Okay, see you later," I said as I folded up the cloth.

Dad came out of the garage.

"Suzu...what about dinner tonight?" he asked.

I slung my bag on my shoulder and shook my head without looking him in the eye.

"How about I make tataki?"

I shook my head again.

"Oh… Okay," he said, then got in his car and left for work.

Dad and I have an awkward conversation like this every morning.

I hurried across the bridge, scrolling through news on my phone:

Belle Cancels Concert After Unexpected Incident

"Ugh, I'm sorry…"

I hated having disappointed everyone who'd been looking forward to that show. I was thinking about how I should prepare better next time, when I tripped over a dent in the bridge and stumbled forward.

"Ack!"

I made a valiant effort to hold myself up by flapping my arms but sadly ended up flat on my face.

"Oof! Owwww…!!"

A red bump quickly formed on my forehead. On the screen of my dropped phone, a red mark appeared on Belle's forehead, too. My device had detected the inflammation. U's body-sharing technology linked me to Belle through my biometric info.

"It wasn't Belle's fault!"

Hiro's shrill pronouncement echoed into the hallway.

"It was all the Dragon! I seriously wish they'd just unveil him already!!"

By afternoon, the bump on my forehead had gone down quite a bit.

"I wonder why he upsets people on purpose like that," I mused, probing the bump.

"He's just showing off!" Hiro said, scribbling the answer to a physics problem on the whiteboard like she was letting off steam. Mr. Terada had left it there on purpose as a challenge to his students, and Hiro had accepted.

"He might have some reason."

"It's all a bluff!"

"You think?" I wasn't entirely convinced.

"Why don't we figure out who he is and unveil him ourselves?"

Hiro finished writing the answer, then underlined it forcefully with a double line as if to say she'd solve whatever problem Mr. Terada served up.

We bumped into Kamishin on the way out of the classroom.

"Oh, hi, Suzu."

"What's with the big backpack?" I asked. He looked fitted out for a camping trip or something.

"I've got an away game."

"A game?"

Just then, Hiro squeezed out the door with a bulky cardboard-wrapped package loaded onto a metal carrying frame on her back.

"You too, Hiroka?" Kamishin asked.

"Don't lump me in with you!" she snapped back.

Hiro and I left school and got on the train. She heaved her oversized package onto a seat, then immediately took her iPad out of her tote bag and started explaining things.

"ASes are linked to a person's biometric data that's constantly being scanned by their device, so a single user can't have two ASes."

"Right."

"Plus, I searched the whole net, and there's zero info about the

Dragon out there other than that he showed up at U's martial arts hall—no nationality, no age, no gender, nothing."

"Then how are we going to find him?"

"There might not be info about the Dragon himself, but there are records of everyone he's fought so far."

"Aha!"

"In the past seven months, he's won three hundred and sixty-nine fights, lost three, and tied two. Most of these three hundred and seventy-four individuals have other social media accounts linked to their U account. We might figure something out if we talk to them all."

We got off the train, boarded the bus, and took it to my stop, where we walked along the Niyodo until we came to my old elementary school, nestled in the green summer mountains. The same abandoned school the women's choir used for practice.

I pointed Hiro up to a classroom on the second floor. Despite her heavy-looking pack, she sprang up the stairs energetically.

A lot of schools that close because of population loss and rural decline are simply left as they were, or else turned into slowly moldering storage spaces. A minority are turned into dormitories or activity centers. Ours, fortunately enough, became a community center. I filled out a room-use form at the front desk.

"We're going to use it for studying," I told the attendant.

Then I got a laundry list of rules. You're allowed to use the stuff in the rooms, but please share it with others. In case of an earthquake, remember to put on one of the safety helmets before evacuating. Et cetera, et cetera. Once that was done, I went up to the classroom.

"...Oh!"

I looked around in surprise. A whole array of monitors had been set up around a central large screen. It was like a secret intelligence headquarters. Hiro had hooked up the unused school equipment to her own high-performance computer tower, which is what she'd been carrying in the cardboard wrapping. While I was signing up for the room, she'd managed to set up her entire living-room system.

"You're amazing!" I couldn't help moaning.

She flashed me a proud, toothy smile. "Hee-hee-hee-hee!"

On the main monitor, the Dragon's 374 opponents were pinpointed on a world map. Hiro addressed all of them at once.

"I have a question for everyone who's fought the Dragon. Who is he?"

An icon near Philadelphia popped up. It was a brawny wrestler AS wearing a tiger mask.

"He's a mystery. Definitely not an AI, though."

The icon flipped over to reveal a slender boy holding a cat—completely different from his AS. He was frank with us.

Near the Strait of Dover, in France, a hefty green goblin fighter AS popped up.

"Super aggressive. The worst."

The icon flipped to reveal a cheerful young blond girl.

Near Mumbai, India, an AS that looked like the divine bird Garuda appeared, tilting its head in puzzlement.

"I don't know why he goes that far."

The real person behind the AS was a young, intelligent-looking doctor wearing glasses.

Near Shenzhen, China, an AS that looked like the Stone Man answered:

"I was one of his first opponents. He didn't have as many bruises back then."

The real person was a kindly middle-aged police officer.

"So the bruises came from all the fights?" I asked the screen.

Hiro focused in on the three people who had defeated the Dragon.

"Here's a question for the few of you who beat him. How did you win?"

"He got sloppy all of a sudden," a boy in Los Angeles answered.

"I think he got distracted," a thirty-something woman from Moscow added.

Of course, not everyone who fought him made their location public. The third winning combatant was among them.

"The angel…," I murmured. It was the AS who had cheered Belle up that first snowy night.

"What about you? Do you have anything to add?" Hiro asked. The angel put out a wordless comment bubble:

…………

Then the icon vanished from the screen altogether.

"Ah!"

It was gone. Hiro's slightly sharp tone must have scared it off. She was irritated.

"Argh! Not even a rumor?"

Who knows…?

Could be him.

You think?

The bruises look the same

An intricate web of answers popped up one after the next.

"Who is 'him'?"

Several links appeared, and Hiro clicked one of them. It opened the browser and displayed a bunch of image search results. One of those results was a young Caucasian man glaring sharply at the camera.

"His name's Jelinek," said Hiro. "An obscure contemporary artist."

His long, black hair streaked with highlights fit my mental image of an artist.

We clicked through to his website. The home page had a photo of him showing off a tattoo on his pale white skin, displayed like it was one of his own creations. True enough, the color and shape were surprisingly similar to the bruises on the Dragon's back. The tattoo was on the man's back, too.

Images from various social media platforms were embedded in the website. Pictures of his paintings, a woman in glasses—probably his girlfriend—which was all well and good…but for some reason, there were also pictures of a car crash and a graveyard. Why would someone want the whole world to see this stuff? So creepy.

"Six months ago, he started getting tattoos of bruises all over his body. That fits with when the Dragon joined U. After that, the value of his artwork increased twentyfold," Hiro announced.

"Very fishy…," I groaned. I would never want to talk to this man, or have anything to do with him.

"Oh."

"What?"

"His agent's number is listed here."

"It is?"

"I'm cold-calling them."

"What? Really? Hey!"

Before I could tell her to wait, Hiro had pressed the call button on her video chat app, which promptly started ringing. *Crap, now what? I was literally just thinking about how I never want to talk to him!*

The agent connected Jelinek to the call. It was late afternoon for us, night for him.

"*I have nothing to say,*" he said crossly from his studio. His irritation was palpable even through the machine translation. Given his paint-spattered apron and the brush in his hand, he must have been in the middle of painting. I thought I glimpsed a tattoo peeking out from the sleeve of his T-shirt; it looked like one of the Dragon's bruises.

"What do your tattoos mean?" Hiro asked point-blank in a strange voice.

"Just who the hell are you people?!"

"What were you doing last night?" she went on. His outburst didn't ruffle her.

The video app automatically displayed our screen next to his. There we were, all blown up and larger than life: two weird girls wearing hard hats and large surgical masks, with our bangs in our eyes and our hands folded in front of our noses. His reaction wasn't surprising.

He shook his head in exasperation, then suddenly gave in to his anger and blocked the screen with his hand.

"Get a life!"

"Why won't you answer my questions?"

"Shut up!"

His screen went black. A message appeared saying he'd left the chat. We took off our masks.

"He's definitely hiding something," Hiro muttered.

The conversation replayed in slow motion. An enlarged version of Jelinek's nasty expression as he blocked the screen leered at us.

We continued our global search from the abandoned school the next day. I made a pot of the black tea I'd brought from home and put a tea cozy over it. Hiro sipped from a cup while she interviewed the ASes.

"Can you think of anyone else?"

Dunno

I know someone kind of like that.

Someone just as annoying

That lady who's always saying she's been hurt

Yeah, it could be her.

"Her?" I asked, looking up. So the Dragon wasn't necessarily male.

Hiro did an image search. A heavyset, middle-aged Asian woman with a mean-looking expression appeared. She was wearing a fur coat and sunglasses. Her teeth were bared in a menacing smile.

"Her name is Swan. Has a bunch of different social media accounts and is known for her pushy, argumentative comments and crazy outbursts," Hiro explained. "'That hurt me' is like her catchphrase. She relentlessly drives people into a corner—that certainly sounds like a monster."

Lots of screenshots of Swan's comments on social media came up in our search, written in English, Chinese, and Malay. I couldn't read them, but somehow I could tell they were really awful.

"Yikes…"

"Ooh, found her meeting ID."

"What?!"

"I'm calling her," Hiro said, taking off her uniform necktie.

"Wait! Wait a minute!"

I set down my tea and frantically searched for something to disguise myself with. *Ack, no hard hats in here today!*

Hiro swiftly pulled her hair back, put on a pair of black-rimmed glasses, and swiped on some lipstick. I had nothing.

Crap!

I heard the ringtone.

Help!

Swan appeared in the video chat.

Her face looked totally different from the photos we'd seen online. She spoke politely and had an elegance to her. I might even call her modest. She had black hair and silver-rimmed glasses. Her sleeveless dress was showy but attractive. Behind her in the high-ceilinged kitchen, I could see a dining table big enough to seat twenty people, set with dishes, glasses, and flower arrangements.

"*I was at a birthday party that day,*" Swan said with a gentle smile.

"A birthday party?" asked Hiro, pretending to be a magazine editor.

"Yes, for my husband. I was so busy preparing, and then my daughters helped bake the cake."

"Oh, I'm looking at the pictures right now."

"Are you?"

A picture on her social media feed showed her two young daughters holding up the cake. Scrolling down, another showed them clinging to their fashionable father, who sported a tidy goatee.

"Your family looks very close."

"*Are you sure I'm the one you want for your article on 'the ideal housewife'?*" Swan asked hesitantly.

"Oh yes," Hiro answered solicitously. "Our readers are going to adore you. I'll be in touch once I have further details."

She ended the call. I looked up in relief from the tea cozy I'd placed over my head as a disguise.

"She didn't seem scary at all," I mentioned.

"Everything she just said was a lie." Hiro shook her hair loose and removed her earrings. "She doesn't have a husband or daughters, and she didn't make the cake; she had it delivered."

"What?!"

"The live feed from outside her house hasn't shown anything but Amazon and Uber Eats delivery people for months. Everything she posts on her social media are stock photos. Like this one, and this one, and this one."

The freshly baked cake, the two young daughters, the fashionable husband… All of it was part of the fake family this fabulously wealthy woman pretended lived with her in that big house. A shiver ran down my spine.

"Freaky… Why would she do that?"

This was the woman who frequented social media sites around the world writing "You hurt me" in all different languages. Hiro offered her level-headed analysis.

"She doesn't have an alibi, and she's extremely aggressive. If the bruises represent her comments…she could be the Dragon."

Wounds… Bruises on the Dragon's back… Maybe.

We found an anonymous message board with a thread titled "Searching for the Dragon's identity," but it wasn't clear if anything the people were saying was true.

How much do I have to pay the Justices to get an item that lets me unveil other people?

Idiot, they don't sell those items. That's what's wrong with the system.

Why do they have more power than the rest of us?

Voices, can you fix that please?

After the Beast is unveiled

A ballpark in Anaheim, California.

In the right-side batter's box, Fox, an outfielder for the Wildebeests, cracked his bat hard against a well-placed ball with a slight uppercut swing.

"Whoo-hoo!!"

The crowd roared with approval.

"As his performance in last year's World Series showed, Fox is one of MLB's strongest hitters. He's extremely popular with the fans, but rumor has it he's hiding a horrible secret," the aging commentator said, like he was showing off a brand-new possession.

"A rumor?" The announcer of the long-running program egged him on.

A large monitor in the TV studio displayed Fox's handsome, bearded face looking up as he hit a home run. The commentator lowered his voice intimately.

"He plays the gentleman, but underneath the mask is a violent man."

The image on the monitor transitioned from a shot of Fox sliding for a catch to one showing the team practicing. Everyone was talking casually in T-shirts under the bright sun, except for Fox. He was going for a run all by himself in a long-sleeved hooded sweatshirt, clearly the odd man out.

"They say he never takes off his top during practice because he's covered in huge scars."

"Wowww..."

Astounded, nervous murmurs ran through the studio audience.

Huge scars? That was hard to believe. Why? Was he a dangerous man? What kind of wounds did he have?

The announcer voiced those feelings.

"Every superstar has skeletons in their closet. We're disillusioned every time we discover them."

"Ohhh..."

A murmur of satisfaction and reassurance passed through the crowd. Of course every celebrity had a side the public wasn't aware of. That was a given. I doubt anyone would be surprised if he was eventually arrested for some sort of violent offense. They'd probably tell their friends and family they thought he was suspicious from the start.

Fox was flashing a brilliant smile on the monitor.

Hiro had taped the show and replayed it for me. I gazed at Fox's blue eyes.

There were several big bruises under them.

The commentator's words echoed in my mind.

Scars…

Could he be the one…?

"Hiya, it's Hey-o Doggo here."

"And Mr. Reseggnation."

Hey-o Doggo was a weak-looking dog wearing a T-shirt. Mr. Reseggnation was the egg character with the crack in his head. The two of them had a YouTube channel.

"Did you hear?" Hey-o Doggo asked Mr. Reseggnation.

"About what?"

"There's a new AS popular with kids."

"Wait, more popular than me? Who is it? Tell me, tell me!"

"*You're* popular? You've been around since 1990!"

A picture of the Dragon appeared onscreen. Both characters fell over.

"Whoa!!"

"I'm talking about the Dragon."

"I thought everyone hated him."

Mr. Reseggnation punched the picture of the Dragon.

Right away, comments from kids all around the world showed up.

The program was being broadcast live, and two kids were chosen at a time to talk on the stream. Hey-o Doggo read out their names and ages.

"We've got Aileen, who's thirteen, and Omari, who's ten."

The kids explained excitedly why they liked the Dragon.

"The Dragon's lair is called the Castle."

"We're competing to see who can find it first."

Hey-o Doggo read out the names of the next children.

"Here we've got Camille, age sixteen, and Jake, age thirteen."

"What'll you do if you find it?" Mr. Reseggnation asked them.

"Take a selfie with him!"

"Shake his hand!"

"Next, Charlie, age eighteen, and Leo, age nine."

"He's a bad guy, right?"

"That's why he's the coolest."

"I like how he's quiet but strong."

"Now we have Tomo, who's eleven, and Kei, who's fourteen."

"You don't think he's scary?"

"The Dragon...is...my hero." The pale-faced boy named Tomo was tilting his head for some reason.

"Does your neck hurt?"

He glanced around nervously with vacant eyes. He didn't seem quite like all the other kids. Mr. Reseggnation turned to Kei, who was dressed in black.

"Hey, you in the back, look over here."

But Kei refused to look at him.

I was watching the broadcast in bed.

"A hero..."

So the Dragon everyone on social media hated was a hero to the kids. What was the truth?

I stopped the livestream, and a series of related videos appeared. I found one featuring the kid called Tomo and clicked it.

"Yes, we're a happy little family of three. We're doing just fine without Mom around."

A reliable-looking, confident man with thick eyebrows had his arms around Tomo's and Kei's shoulders. He must be their father. Tomo had the same vacant look in his eyes and kept twining his fingers together. Kei, still wearing black, was looking down silently.

Guess there's all sorts of families out there. Mine included. But we're not a happy little family, and we're not "doing just fine."

"We support each other and we enjoy every day."

In the video, the father looked back and forth between his sons, smiling. They didn't say anything.

Dad and I didn't support each other.

On another channel, a poor-looking young guy was streaming from his bedroom.

"We've been buddies for ages," he said, holding up a picture of the Dragon on his phone.

On this one creepy channel, a young man wearing the head of a mascot costume was shaking his head like he was dizzy.

"Me and the Dragon are hella tight."

One of the naughtier channels had several young women in sexy bathing suits lounging on a king-size bed under a pink light.

"He's actually crazy rich. Keep up the clicks if you wanna see his super luxurious mansion," one of them said, shaking her rear end provocatively.

Comments kept popping up in one corner of the screen:

They're all full of crap

Don't believe any of it.

Click here for the real story →

Day by day, more people were claiming to be friends with the Dragon or to know his secrets. The web was becoming a tangle of questionable information about him.

Who's the Dragon?

Yeah, who?

Who is he?

Who?

Rumors about him were spreading like crazy. The endless glittering streets of U buzzed with the ever-growing chatter of ASes.

Who's behind the Dragon?

Who is he?

Who?

Who...?

THE DRAGON'S CASTLE

My elderly neighbors were chatting noisily. A mobile market had been set up in the parking lot of the Hometown Center, and everyone was here doing their grocery shopping. Hometown Centers are local activity centers that sell local specialty items and stuff like that. They've got them in villages all over the prefecture, but they're run independently by each community. They sell food, too.

Today the whiteboard menu read LUNCH SPECIAL: ¥400.

Hiro and I had set up camp in the back of the cafeteria. She'd been a huge fan of this place ever since I took her there for the first time. She held up two fingers like she was a regular.

"Hi, Mrs. Tsutsui. Two lunch specials, please."

"Coming right up," Mrs. Tsutsui said, walking off to the kitchen, her back hunched as always. She's the best cook. Once, in elementary school, I asked her how old she was and she said 85. She says the same thing when I ask her now. She's so energetic I can't even second-guess her.

While we waited for our food, Hiro showed me a news video on her phone. Jelinek was speaking solemnly to a large crowd of reporters.

"It's absolutely not a publicity stunt. I lost the love of my life in an accident and I'm still grieving. I got my tattoos in the same places she was injured."

Weeping, he kneeled in front of a gravestone and covered his face. A flock of cameras were trained on him.

I remembered the photo of a graveyard on his website. This was the same place. The picture of the awful car accident must have been where the woman with the glasses died. I stared in surprise at this unexpectedly sentimental man.

"Wow, seems like everyone's got big secrets," I said, meaning it. But Hiro rolled her eyes.

"You're so gullible. He's just saying that to hide an even bigger secret."

"You're such a skeptic."

"Of course I am. The question is, what is he hiding?"

"Everyone has secrets."

"Including you."

"And you."

"Me? I'm an open book."

"Then what about the wallpaper on your phone?"

Hiro suddenly turned bright red. "Hey, that's not fair!"

"That picture of Mr. Terada from physics class?"

"Shhh, someone might hear you!" she whispered, hugging her phone to her chest. Just then, Mrs. Tsutsui arrived with our meals.

"Here you go, ladies."

Hiro's wallpaper was a photo of Mr. Terada standing in front of a blackboard covered in solved physics problems.

"I'm a nobody to him," she said, her hands pressed to her flushed cheeks. "You better not tell my parents. They think I'm such a good girl."

"I won't say anything."

"My mom would keel over if she knew. The other day—"

She stopped suddenly.

"Sorry," she said.

"It's fine."

"I'm really sorry," she repeated guiltily, her hand over her mouth.

"Seriously, it's fine. I was just thinking about how you actually talk to your parents."

I stared at my lunch special. There was some vegetable tempura, simmered beans and tofu, a bowl of vegetable soup, and some greens. A full meal.

"I'm the total opposite. Ever since my mom died, it's just been me and my dad, but we hardly ever talk to each other."

I avoided looking at him whenever possible. He kept his distance, too, out of consideration for me. But was this really what we wanted? To eat separately even though it was just the two of us?

Hiro stared at me, then mumbled, "I know… That's why I'm here with you."

Then she picked up her chopsticks and started wolfing down her lunch. Very loudly.

"Hey, stop moping and eat your food," she said.

I picked up my chopsticks and nibbled at my meal. Her mouth crammed full, Hiro turned around, raised two fingers, and called, "Excuse me, ma'am! Two orders of somen noodles, please!!"

"Of course," Mrs. Tsutsui called back, sticking her head out of the kitchen. Her somen is out of this world.

Hiro's AS caught wind of some new information.

If you leave U's riverlike Main Stream and head up toward the sea of clouds, you'll see lots of little floating islands. People say they're units that operated in U's early days, the wreckage of old internet services that were shut down. One of them is supposedly the Dragon's castle.

I pulled my hood up and approached a suspicious-looking island.

"Yikes!"

Glimpsing several figures, I slipped into the shadow of a column. They were Justice troops. They seemed to be searching for something, but eventually they went off somewhere else. Maybe they'd heard the same rumor as Hiro and come searching for the Dragon. I emerged from behind the column and looked around.

"...Is there really a castle among these ruins?" I asked Hiro.

"This time I'm sure of it!"

"Then why won't you come with me?"

Her AS had stayed behind.

"I've got an extra lesson with Mr. Terada. I'll watch the video later. Seeya!"

"Gimme a break..."

Like the Main Stream, the units were made up of two basic elements, skyscrapers and parks. Of course, the parks didn't have any real greenery. There were rows of conifer-like pyramids in a plaza paved with round tiles. They were missing in several places, which really chipped away at the whole 3D feel. Strolling through these ruins, I presently came to the gate of a skyscraper district and passed through.

"Looking for something?" a voice suddenly asked.

A form was peering at me from the center of the main street threading between abandoned buildings: a bizarre cross between a pretty girl and a white sea slug. It hovered gently in midair. I wasn't sure if it was a sea slug with the face of a pretty girl or a pretty girl with the body of a sea slug.

"...Who are you?" I asked.

"I'm an AI. I know everything."

She had a cute starfish clip in her pink hair. I guess you could consider her a mermaid.

"...I'm looking for a castle," I asked experimentally.

The mermaid AI smiled, waving the feelers on her back like she was swimming.

"I thought so."

"You did...?"

Suddenly, the landscape morphed around her. I found myself standing on the edge of a lagoon fed by a magnificent waterfall.

"...It's here?"

This was where his castle was?

But the mermaid just waved her feelers and swam silently away.

"No, wait!"

I tried following only to quickly lose sight of her.

"Where am I...?"

It was nearly impossible to walk through the tangle of tree trunks and roots. They seemed to be blocking the way forward. I stumbled lost through the deep primeval forest.

I was panting and sweating beneath my heavy coat. My hood got caught on the branches.

Of course, there was no path. I had no idea where I would end up. But if I didn't keep moving, I could never hope to escape this maze. My only choice was to move forward into the unknown.

"Huff... Huff..."

I emerged in front of a strange tree whose trunk and branches were intertwined around a huge rock. I didn't know if the tree was embracing the rock or strangling it. I stopped, unsure what to do.

"May I help you?" a voice said.

"...Oh!"

This time the peculiar creature looking at me was a cross between a pretty girl and a squilla shrimp. Another mermaid. She had thick, curly green hair and a frilly tutu-like thing around her waist. Another AI?

"...I'm looking for a castle," I tried venturing again.

The mermaid smiled, waving her six legs.

`"I thought so. I will tell only you."`

"Um..."

Before I could say anything, I was whisked off to another place. This time I was at the seashore. As far as my eyes could see, there was nothing but the shallow, utterly flat edge of the ocean. A strong wind was blowing.

I stepped from the damp sand onto the water's mirrorlike surface, dotted with reflections of clouds. I didn't know which direction to go. Whichever way I looked, all I saw was the horizon dividing the sky from the sea and land.

I walked on and on, breathing hard. I wasn't even sure if I was moving forward. I got the feeling I was lost again. It was far easier to walk here than in that primeval forest, but wherever I went my surroundings looked the same. I began to feel driven into a mental corner, like I was expending needless energy.

"*Huff... Huff...* Where am I?"

Did this castle even exist?

`"May I help you?"`

Again, I suddenly heard a voice.

Colorful seashells had been stacked on the beach. From their shadow, a peculiar creature resembling a cross between a pretty girl and a sea anemone was peering out at me.

"Uh..."

Her small face poked out from a soft-looking pink body. On the opposite side were four fingers whose tips were adorned with nail art. Before I could ask my question, the mermaid said perceptively, "You're looking for the castle, aren't you? Don't tell anyone else!"

"Wait!" I called after her, but I was too late. I was surrounded by pure white clouds. "Oh! Where am I?"

Since everything was white, I didn't even know which way was up. I was worse than lost. A horrible anxiety overcame me.

"I can't see a thing! Ugh…"

Would I simply disappear? I started panicking.

"How silly. You got tricked," a voice said.

"Huh?!" I whipped my head around. "…Oh!"

A creature was floating in the sea of clouds.

It was the angel AS. It flapped its soft white wings.

"You'll never find it at this rate."

"You…know about the castle?"

"Don't worry about that. Play with me instead."

The clouds gradually cleared to reveal a vista of mountains. A narrow path climbed a sunny slope into the distance.

"Follow me up this path," the angel AS said, twirling invitingly into the distance.

"Hey, wait!!"

I hurried after. Far above the mountains, beyond the towering clouds, an enormous form lurked. I stared at it. The clouds continued to clear. Between them, I could see what looked like a building. *What is that?*

Its bizarre form was covered in strange markings.

"…The castle!!"

* * *

Could this really be the Dragon's castle, like Hiro had told me? I placed my hand on the huge door, still unsure.

Crrreak…

It opened just a crack. The angel AS slipped through.

Should I follow?

I can't say I didn't hesitate. But I'd set out to find the castle, and I'd gone through a lot to get this far. I summoned my courage and pushed the door all the way open.

Crrrrreak…

"Hello? Is anyone here?" I called.

The place seemed abandoned. I squinted into the darkness, and slowly, my eyes adjusted. My heels clicked across a marble floor inlaid with a lattice pattern. A sweeping staircase rose from the center of the high-ceilinged entrance hall, like you'd see in a medieval castle.

"Wow…" I couldn't help gasping as I stared up at it.

But as I looked closer, I noticed bizarre forms carved into the ceiling and thick, sturdy pillars. It wasn't a classic medieval castle after all. Here and there, I spotted what looked like digital noise. Maybe the castle had been abandoned when its data got corrupted.

"Hurry," the angel AS said from the top of the stairs. I ran after it.

Somewhere nearby, I heard girls whispering.

"Why is she here?"

"We tried to stop her…"

It was the mermaids who had sent me in the wrong direction. They were hiding behind a column on the balcony. I was sure of it.

As I walked down a long hallway, I heard whispers again. They were behind a scary-looking statue.

"What should we do?"

"Master will be furious…"

I kept walking, pretending not to hear.

I followed the angel AS into a courtyard. In the center was a squared-off pillar, like an obelisk, but halfway up it broke into spinning pixelated cubes. More corrupted data. But my eyes were drawn by something else.

Roses.

Roses blooming wildly in these digital ruins.

"...They're beautiful."

They were just like real roses. White, red, pink, crimson, even black. I pulled back my hood and walked up to them. Their unmistakable sweet fragrance filled my nostrils.

"I grew them," the angel AS said, as if it couldn't resist boasting. "My secret roses..."

"Secret?" I echoed, taking one in my hand. "What kind of secret?"

In place of an answer, I heard a monster's roar behind me.

I looked around in surprise. The Dragon emerged from the shadow of a pillar.

"What are you doing here?!"

"Oh...!"

I was too shocked to move. With an irritated scowl, the Dragon circled around and stepped between me and the roses.

"Why did you enter without permission?!"

"I... It brought me here—"

"Leave!!" the Dragon shouted without letting me finish.

"But—"

"Leave!!" he said again, then vanished from the courtyard.

I stood rooted to the spot, my knees shaking. Finally, I shook my head, forcing myself back to my senses.

"...Wait!" I called, chasing the Dragon down the long hallway. "I came here because I wanted to ask you something!"

The Dragon was wearing tattered old clothes. Still, his countless wounds were marked in the same places they had been the day he wore the red cape. It seemed the data for the wounds was displayed even when he changed clothes.

"Who are you? Who…?"

But the Dragon kept striding forward until he emerged into a large room.

"Answer me!" I called. Suddenly, he turned and screamed at me, a terrifying look in his eyes.

"Get out, or I will rip you to pieces!!"

His voice echoed across the crumbling ballroom. I trembled in fear that he really would rip me apart with those sharp teeth. Still, I gathered my courage and stared him dead in the eye, determined not to lose this battle, at least in spirit.

"Hnnn…"

Just then, I heard what sounded like a whining puppy. It was the angel AS.

It drifted toward us like a falling autumn leaf, then flew away as if blown by the wind.

"Where are you going…?" the Dragon asked worriedly, chasing after the angel. His voice was unrecognizable from the one he'd used with me a moment before. I didn't know what to think.

The angel only whimpered in response.

"Wait," the Dragon called.

The ballroom had twelve round gates in a circle, each with a distinctive mark drawn above it. Still whimpering, the angel left through a gate with a spiral mark. The Dragon followed. I followed the Dragon.

I craned my neck up as we climbed a cracked spiral staircase. It was pixelated in several places where the data was corrupted. At the very top was a balcony. Part of the exterior wall's data was visible, as if the building had been abandoned halfway through construction. The angel AS floated outside the balcony, sniffling.

"Wait...," the Dragon said, leaning so far over the balcony I thought he might fall. He cupped the angel AS gently between his hands, then carefully brought it toward him so as not to hurt it. When he opened his hands, the angel's chest was blinking like a heartbeat.

"Trouble...? Are we in trouble...?" the angel asked in a barely audible voice.

"No, it's fine... Everything is fine," the Dragon answered, his voice tender. I glimpsed a sensitive thoughtfulness completely opposite from his fearsome appearance. I stared at him from behind.

Before I knew what I was doing, I asked, "Which is it?"

"......?"

The Dragon looked back at me with sharp, questioning eyes.

"Which one is the real you?" I asked directly.

"......"

Without answering, he walked away. I ran after him as he strode briskly down the hallway.

"Wait!" I called.

He turned a corner, opened a large door, and entered a room.

"Stop!!"

Just before I reached the door, he slammed it with a *bang*.

"......"

I rested my hand on it, at a loss.

I was thinking about the Dragon. Who was he, really?

LOVE

"Suzu's in love. And with a bad boy, too," Ms. Nakai abruptly announced one day during a break in choir practice.

"...Wh-whaaaat?!"

I'd been thinking back on what happened at the Dragon's castle, my hand resting on the upright piano and my head in a daze. I blushed and protested incoherently.

"No—no way. Why do you think that...?!"

"It's written all over your face," Ms. Nakai said, like a detective pointing to a smoking gun. I covered my bright red face with my hands.

All five of the choir members were seated on a bench, grinning.

"Teen girls just love bad boys," Ms. Kita said, flapping her fan.

"'He's so sweet and lonely deep down,'" Ms. Okumoto teased, grasping the back of the bench with both hands.

"'I'm the only one who understands him!'" Ms. Nakai added, lowering her teacup momentarily. They all exchanged glances and laughed.

"I said you're wrong!!"

I knew they were teasing me, but I couldn't help protesting. Of course, my denials probably just further convinced them they were right.

"How about giving him a present?" Ms. Hatanaka suggested helpfully.

"Huh?"

"I studied abroad in Ohio in my last year of high school. There was this one boy with these penetrating eyes, always by himself. He seemed lonely."

"The lone-wolf type?" Ms. Kita asked, covering her mouth with her fan and widening her eyes like a doe-eyed maiden.

Ms. Hatanaka shrugged. "I was kind of interested in him, so I decided to give him a birthday present."

"What did you give him?"

"A song."

"A song?" the other ladies echoed in unison.

Ms. Hatanaka looked at me. "A birthday song. I wrote it and sang it to him."

"That's so beautiful," Ms. Yoshitani said, pressing her hands to her chest.

"A love song!"

"That was the first time I saw him smile. He said he was happy."

"Did you two date?"

"Goodness, no!"

"Why not?"

"He was only in eighth grade!"

"No way!" they cried.

"He cried at the airport when I went home. It was sweet."

I gazed at Ms. Hatanaka's beautiful profile. I'm sure she was gorgeous in high school. I wondered what ever happened to the junior high boy. Did he still remember the present she gave him?

* * *

As I walked along the Kagami River on my way home from school, a thought occurred to me.

"I've never written a love song before..."

I looked up and glanced around searchingly. The river was calm that day. True to its name, it reflected the nearby buildings like a mirror. Several children were playing on the far bank; a few women were playing badminton. Cars were parked outside Yamauchi Shrine. Elderly couples were leisurely ambling along. Bicycles passed me by.

Fragments of everyday life. Could I find hidden beauty in the road I was so used to walking?

I followed a pair of wagtails with my eyes as they skimmed the river's surface. As I watched them fly, a melody came to me. The wagtails rose from the river, switching places in the air. I felt myself becoming freer as I observed them.

I craned my neck, squinting into the afternoon sun. I could see Shinobu behind my closed eyes. He was on the basketball court.

A lazy six-eight beat. I stepped in time, getting excited.

Another image of Shinobu came to me. The sensation of his hand squeezing mine.

The feeling of slowly soaring down a river.

The Dragon appeared in my mind's eye. He was gazing sharply up at me.

I lifted my heels and did a pirouette.

Another image of the Dragon. His sensitive, kind voice.

I—no, Belle—couldn't stop thinking about him. That was the truth.

But could I call it love, like Ms. Nakai had?

I didn't know.

Love.

I'd never had anything to do with romance up till now.

But there was a place in my heart I'd always kept hidden.

A feeling I'd always had.

Did this come from the same place?

If it did—

But was it worth anything?

Could I—?

But it didn't matter. I felt free.

I put my heart into the melody.

I let the sensation linger, then opened my eyes.

Somehow, I was at the aqueduct just before Yanagihara Bridge.

I nodded to myself. It wasn't half bad. It was a quiet, sad kind of song, but among the better ones I'd written lately.

"Might as well record it," I mumbled to myself.

I swiped from my phone's home screen until I got to the song-writing app—but suddenly, my fingers froze.

"…Huh?"

I swiped back to the home screen. The red circle at the top right corner of the messaging app showed an unusual number of notifications. 200, 250, 300…

"So many…," I muttered, tapping it. An avalanche of messages appeared.

I saw her holding hands with Shinobu

Is she showing off?

Why her though?

Apparently they're old friends

That doesn't mean she can get away with whatever she wants!

Girl thinks she's hot stuff. She should stay in her lane

"What in the world…?!"

Rumors about me were flying fast and thick in the high school girls' group chat I belonged to. The blood drained from my face. My hand shook as it gripped the phone. Was I about to be excommunicated?

Oh crap!

I straightened up, spun around, and started running like my life depended on it.

What do I do?

My phone buzzed. A phone call at a time like this?

"Suzu!"

"Hiro!!"

"You didn't tell Shinobu you liked him, did you?!"

"No, I didn't!!"

"Did he tell you he does?"

"Of course not!!"

"So why...?"

"We just—"

"Held hands?!"

This was a battlefield.

A wasteland where speculation, suspicion, selfishness, and hatred tangled together both inside and outside the group. All at once, in the forests, fields, villages, rivers, and beaches of the battle map, the figurines of the girls in my class spun around, revealing different faces.

All of them were furious.

"I didn't hold his hand! He just grabbed mine!!" I insisted, trying to defend myself, but the girls kept hurling themselves against me one after another, and my hit points kept going down.

"That's all?! Now it's blown up. Shinobu must really be something. It goes to show how he's on basically everyone's radar," Hiro pointed out.

"I didn't even do anything!!"

"This is spreading like wildfire. It's like all the girls who flirted with him and all the ones who didn't but wanted to suddenly stopped holding back and everything just exploded. This place is a real hornet's nest. It's scary."

Scuffles were breaking out everywhere. They were all basically the same, but some developed into battles. Knights on horseback leered at each other, their flags flying high. On other fields, troops armed with guns stared each other down. And on others, bigger platoons armed with bigger guns were a hair's breadth from all-out war.

"But everyone used to be friends!" I protested.

"You never really know, I guess. If they keep showing their true colors, we're gonna have a full-blown war."

"What should we do?"

"I suppose I have no choice."

Hiro's figurine burrowed into the ground of the battle map and circled around to the bottom of the field.

"I'll figure out a game plan and shake things up. You try talking some sense into the more rational girls!"

"I'll do my best!"

Hiro's trap made of words sent one figurine after the next flying. The battlefield was in chaos. Without pausing for breath, she moved on to destabilize the next group. Hiro was the type to strike hard and fast. Meanwhile, I gathered the courage to approach one group of girls.

"Listen to me! Shinobu's just a childhood friend!"

I moved on to another group.

"He was treating me like a little kid!"

I pleaded my case desperately.

"He would never date someone like me!"

My timing was good. The leaders of the various factions were exhausted from the unexpected battles and leaning toward pacifism anyway. They listened receptively to me.

Good point

Everyone needs to chill.

Yeah, simmer down, ladies

Their figurines flipped once again, showing their ordinary faces.

The revolt was suppressed.

"Hello!" I called, dashing into the entryway of Hiro's house.

"Gah!!" Then I collapsed forward on my face. My phone fell from my hand onto the Persian rug.

"Looks like we managed to escape the lion's den."

Hiro came out to greet me, tablet in hand. Chat notifications from our classmates were blowing up my phone lying on the rug. Hiro leaned against the wall and gave me a sour look.

"Life is harsh. If a sad sack like you tells some guy you like him, all hell breaks loose. If Ruka did the same thing, we'd probably achieve world peace no sweat," she said.

My phone pinged with a text message. I picked it up and looked at what it said.

"It's from Ruka."

"For real?"

"It says, 'Sorry to contact you out of the blue, but there's something I want to ask you.'"

Hiro threw me a suspicious look. "Nice timing. Isn't it weird that she just sent that text?"

"Weird?"

"She might be pulling the strings."

"No way!"

"I bet she's after Shinobu."

"Why would a cute girl like her do a thing like this?"

"She's so bad at that sort of stuff."

"She just said she wants to talk because me and Shinobu are childhood friends."

"Personally, I don't think I'd be mature enough to help her out."

I had no comeback for that. After all, I couldn't rule out the possibility that Hiro's suspicions were right.

I trudged home along the banks of the Kagami River. It was already evening.

The message from Ruka said she wanted to talk to me about someone she liked. I knew I had to respond, but I didn't know what to say.

I was at a loss. My admiration for Ruka kept trading places with suspicion. I wanted to release the suffocating feeling in my chest.

"Urgh! My head's spinning..."

Just then, I heard a splash and looked over at the water.

"......?"

Beneath the setting sun, the long, thin hull of a canoe was gliding over the river's surface toward me.

It was Kamishin. The droplets flying from his paddle drew a clean arc through the air. His movements were sharp and efficient. In a flash, the canoe had passed me.

"...He's really giving it his all," I muttered to myself, only to hear someone answer.

"Sure is. He's a go-getter."

I turned in the speaker's direction as slowly as humanly possible.

"......Shinobu."

"I've been waiting for him, but he just won't call it a day."

Somehow, Shinobu was standing next to me, watching the canoe. I stared up at him, frozen in place.

"Suzu, did something happen today?" he asked casually, still looking into the distance.

"……"

"…You can tell me."

I figured he probably knew about the uproar among the girls earlier in the day. But on second thought, his tone suggested he didn't. Or maybe he did know and was pretending not to.

I had no idea.

I felt like I might be able to ask him something that I normally couldn't. I hesitated, then dove in.

"Actually…there's something I've been wanting to ask you for a long time."

"What is it?" he asked, turning toward me.

"You see…"

I couldn't say it. He very kindly waited as I stared at the ground and stalled.

"It's… Um…"

I pulled myself together and looked up at him.

"I… Oh!"

"Suzu!!"

Just then, Kamishin walked up to us, his canoe over his shoulder.

"You going home now? I just finished practice. Man, I'm beat."

"……"

I was too dazed to react.

"What's wrong?" he asked, trying to read the situation.

I forced my face into a tense smile so he wouldn't guess what was going on.

"Oh, um, Kamishin, your away game—how was it?" I stuttered. That got him going.

"I'm back from the race! And listen to this. I got myself all worked up and took an overnight bus to strut my stuff for the coach at the school I wanna go to, but my time was absolute garbage. Total fail," he said merrily, accompanying his story with overly dramatic gestures and comical poses.

"Oh yeah, look at this!" he went on, pulling a phone in a waterproof case out of his wetsuit and bringing up a photo. It showed a group of high school kids from all over Japan between two tall buildings with some college students. Kamishin was striking a pose in the center of the first row.

"Some of these kids didn't even qualify for the Inter-High Championships like I did, and here I bombed. I felt so bad."

I stared at him, mouth slightly agape.

"You made the championships?"

"Heh-heh, yep," he gloated, scratching his cheek.

Despite the casual way he mentioned it, making it to Inter-High is really impressive. You have to be crazy athletic to single-handedly start up a canoe club one year and make it to the national championships the next.

"Seriously?" I said with the biggest grin I could muster. "That's incredible!! You're awesome!! I'm rooting for you!"

"...Really?" he asked.

"Really!!"

Kamishin seemed to latch onto the phrase "rooting for you." He gazed at me with a serious expression, then turned theatrically to Shinobu.

"So, Shinobu," he said.

"Yeah?"

"Suzu said she's rooting for me. Does that mean..."

"Hmm?"

He placed his hand on his hip with a gentlemanly flourish.

"...maybe she likes me a little?"

My grin vanished. He registered my blank face with a start.

"...Oh, no? ...Maybe not, then," he said very quietly.

Shinobu folded his arms in exasperation. "Go put that thing down already," he said.

"I was just kidding! Anyway, Suzu, thanks for the support!"

"You're welcome."

"Hurry up," Shinobu said.

"Yeah, yeah!"

Kamishin adjusted the canoe on his back and walked barefoot toward the boathouse. Shinobu and I were alone again.

"........."

But despite the perfect opportunity, I couldn't get the words out. Kamishin had ruined my timing. Some sort of balance had crumbled. It wasn't Kamishin's fault; it was my own fault for not being able to take the necessary step. I'd given up on lots of other things for the very same reason: because I couldn't get the timing right. Now I was about to give up again. All I could do was stand rooted to the ground watching the sun set over the river.

After a long silence, Shinobu said, "...So, what were you going to say earlier?"

"...Never mind."

"You're not pushing yourself too hard?"

"Nope."

"Really?"

"Really."

I closed my eyes.

I saw Shinobu's young face peering into my own young face. I had to root out my feelings from back then. I had to squelch the feelings I'd never admitted.

I opened my eyes.

"...Shinobu, you don't have to worry about me anymore."

"Huh?"

I spun on my heel and started walking.

"Suzu!" he called.

I didn't stop. I was feeling more and more pathetic.

"...What am I even trying to do?" I asked myself as I walked away.

Then I started running. My feelings had nowhere to go. I felt like they were going to split me open.

I ran as fast as I could. As I ran, I took out my phone and typed a message to Ruka.

Hi, Ruka, not sure I can be much help, but feel free to ask me anything. I'm here for you.

I sent it.

I stopped to catch my breath, staring at the screen. An answer came right away.

Thanks, Suzu!

Wow, I wasn't expecting that haha. I'll do my best. Thanks for the encouragement!

The cheerful message seemed very Ruka-like. I wondered if "I'm here for you" came across as overly friendly, since we weren't that close. I felt bad for catching her off guard.

My chest felt tight.

As soon as I read the message, tears spilled from my eyes and plopped onto the ground. I wiped them away with the back of my hand. But they just kept coming. My eyes were like leaky faucets I couldn't turn off.

I hugged my phone to my chest and kept on crying.

LOVE SONG

I sat down in the hallway of the Dragon's castle, hugged my chest, and cried. Hurt and sadness overwhelmed me.

When I opened my arms, a round, bruise-like mark appeared on my chest. It emitted a soft, warm light. Just like U's body-sharing technology picks up the inflammatory response caused by physical injuries, I think it must also pick up changes in biometric information caused by emotional wounds and give them physical form.

I heard a *creeeak*. The door opened and the angel AS gestured for me to come in.

I wiped my tears and stood up. The light emanating from my chest faded. The angel AS disappeared into the Dragon's room, as if inviting me to follow. I stepped up to the door and put both hands on it.

I hesitated.

"……"

Then I gathered my resolve and softly pushed.

Creeeeeak…

"…Oh!"

Although it was dark inside, I could see the room was big and stretched far back. The ceiling was high. There was a canopied bed and a large fireplace in the center of one wall. Picking my way between the fragments littering the floor, I looked up at the wall over the fireplace. It was covered in small, framed photographs.

What's this?

There were insects, leaves, flowers, nuts, branches, streams, the wall of a house, a field, clouds… At first glance, the objects all looked ordinary. Nothing about them could help me identify their origin. But the picture in the very middle, in a tall, narrow frame, was different.

"…Who is she?"

It was a picture of a woman in a dress holding a huge bunch of roses. I couldn't make out her expression. A spider's web of cracks extended across the glass over her face.

"……"

How was this woman related to the Dragon? Why was the glass cracked? Had it been cracked to intentionally obscure her face? Or—

I looked around the room, then gasped.

There was the Dragon.

He was sitting on the far side of the messy room, facing the balcony with his back to me. He was very still, perhaps sleeping.

I held my breath and slowly walked toward him, taking care not to make a sound.

"You're hurt…"

For the first time, I saw the bruises covering his large back up close. Their intricate shapes and colors held my eye. Somehow, to me, they were beautiful. What did they mean to the Dragon? I slowly reached out my hand, wanting to find an answer.

Suddenly, he stood and spun around.

"Ah!!" I gasped, shrinking back.

"Don't touch me!!" he yelled nervously. His feelings were very clear.

"I'm sorry. Your bruises…"

"Did you come to laugh at my hideousness?!"

"No!"

I placed my hand over my heart and said, trying to be as empathetic as I could, "Do they hurt? I'm sure they must. You really shouldn't be so violent—"

But the Dragon shook his head before I could finish speaking.

"You don't understand anything."

"Then tell me, so I can understand!"

"Leave!!" he howled, his body shaking like a ferocious beast. "UOOOOOOOOOO!!"

The whole room shook.

I couldn't stay there any longer. I ran out the door and down the hall, turning corner after corner. When I came to the grand entrance hall, the mermaids called out mockingly:

"Go!"

"Leave!"

"Get out!"

I was overcome with humiliation and frustration. But there was nothing more I could do. I left the castle in silence.

I retraced my path, eventually coming to the group of skyscrapers in the abandoned unit. Pulling my hood over my face, I peeked around the corner of one of the buildings, surveying the scene. I saw no one. After another careful check, I scurried forward.

At the corner of another building, I scanned my surroundings several times, then hurried on. On the far side of the wide avenue, I could see a gate dividing a group of tall buildings from a park. Once I made it through that gate, I'd be safely on my way to U's Main Stream.

I heard a voice.

"You there! Wait!"

I froze.

A troop of Justices approached. I was caught just in front of the gate, which I had thought was abandoned. There were a lot of them. They walked up from behind and surrounded me. I kept my back turned and my hood up, hunching my shoulders.

"What are you doing here?" one of them asked.

"Did you see anyone?"

"A hideous monster, perhaps?"

I didn't answer. Instead, I waited for the right moment, then tried to flee. But one of them shot out their hand and violently pulled back my hood. Another hand reached out and grabbed my hair. The ribbon holding it back came undone.

"No!!"

My face was now in full view. All I could do was cover my mouth with my hands.

Someone was standing on the far side of the troops.

"You're…Belle?" the figure asked.

It was Justin. He sounded slightly surprised.

"Why are you here?" he asked.

I glared silently at him.

"You won't answer? Then—"

The bracelet on his right arm glinted, transforming into the winged lion's head.

"Ah…?!"

My heart was pounding out of my chest.

"If you won't tell us, we'll have to see who you really are," Justin said nonchalantly.

He was using the unveiling light to threaten me. I trembled in terror. If my identity was revealed…

"Uh… Uhhh… Uh…!" I stuttered.

At that moment, I glimpsed something hurtle between the buildings toward me.

The Dragon.

Justin glanced down in surprise. "Beast!!"

Suddenly, I was in the Dragon's arms, soaring toward the buildings overhead.

"It's the Beast!"

"Chase him!"

"After him!!"

The Justices followed in hot pursuit.

From my place against his chest, I looked up at the Dragon's face. He was trying to save me? But why? Just a little while ago he'd yelled at me to leave!

Before I knew it, the troops had caught up and were hurling themselves against the Dragon. They kicked his back and punched him, but he did not resist. In the stadium, he had crushed Justices like these so easily, but now, he did nothing.

Taking advantage of his passive response, they amused themselves by punching and kicking him.

Eventually, one asked, "Why won't he fight back?"

"Lost his nerve, has he?" another answered.

"He's gone soft," a third sneered.

"……!" I bit my lip in frustration.

Suddenly, I noticed a skyscraper directly in front of us.

"Oh!"

We were heading straight for it. The Justices were too absorbed in tormenting the Dragon to notice it. The Dragon would be driven into the building.

We sped toward the skyscraper.

"?!"

By the time the Justices realized what was happening, the building was right in front of us. They couldn't swerve. Screaming, they barreled into the thick glass.

The Dragon twisted away in the nick of time, but because he was protecting me, his back hit the glass. He ricocheted off with a loud *thud.*

"GWAAAAAA!" he groaned in pain. Then he began descending, like he had no more energy left to fly. Like a marionette whose strings had been cut, he rocketed downward, scraping against the sides of the buildings. I was afraid he would smash into the ground.

"We'll crash!" I couldn't help screaming.

The Dragon clenched his teeth with effort. Twisting his arched body forward, he nimbly kicked off the building's wall, narrowly avoiding the ground. Still gripping me, he hurtled unsteadily through the chasm between buildings.

"Where's the Dragon?!" I heard Justin yelling, irritated that his troops had lost sight of their prey. "...You beast!!"

The Dragon took me back to his castle in the clouds. Landing softly on the cracked balcony, he carefully set me down. I took a large step away from him. He sank to his knees, exhausted. His breath sounded ragged. I stepped toward him again, worried, only to be sharply repelled.

"Stay back!!" he roared. "Get away from me!"

I obeyed, turning away to leave. But something stopped me. A pain deep in my chest. I pressed my fist against my solar plexus to endure it. Then, unable to defy my feelings, I pursed my lips and turned toward the Dragon.

He was still gasping for breath.

"……"

My chest throbbed with pain. I opened my hand and moved it higher on my chest. Words spilled naturally from my mouth.

"I understand you a little better now."

The Dragon looked up at me, wide-eyed.

I walked up to him and said, "It's right *here* that hurts, isn't it?" as I placed my hand softly on his chest.

"……!" He flinched in surprise. I looked up into his eyes and spoke my thoughts.

"Thank you for saving me."

He brought his face close to mine.

"…Belle."

It was the first time he'd said my name.

The stars began to sparkle.

Slowly, I started singing. My voice echoed across the dark ballroom with its patches of pixelation.

It's easy to push me away from you
Easy to say you want to be left on your own
Yet somehow I can't help but see how
your eyes shy away
Your hands seal the entrance and path to your heart

Anger kept fear and the sadness you feel
under the surface for so long
Locked that room, you keep it inside

Lend me your voice
Words you try so hard to forget,
they'll break through the silence
Bring me close
Let me see the past you regret
deep down below
Show it all

The Dragon listened with his hand on his chest, as if he were looking inward.

Innumerable roses twined over the courtyard. With great care, the angel AS carefully chose a pale pink bloom, then a black one. The mermaids carried them into the ballroom. They approached us, placing the pink rose over my heart. That instant, countless particles of light gathered and then burst apart. A dress made of flower petals drifted down and softly encircled my body. I couldn't help letting out a cry of delight. It was like magic. Sparkling particles of light danced around me.

"Do you like this secret rose?" the angel AS asked proudly, flying up to me.

"It's wonderful," I answered, smiling up at it.

Another group of mermaids placed the black rose over the Dragon's heart. Again, innumerable points of light gathered on the rose and burst apart, transforming into a dashing black suit and cape. The mosaic of bruises emerged on the back of the new cape.

I turned to look at the Dragon.

The Dragon turned to look at me.

Points of light gathered in the crumbling ballroom. As they exploded, the room was transformed into a brilliant, lavish hall.

I held both my hands out to the Dragon in an invitation to dance. But he shrank back, hesitant. I stepped forward encouragingly, my hands still held out. Uncertainly, bashfully, he held up his left hand. I took it in my own.

We paused for a moment, then slowly began twirling.

At first, we were simply holding hands and spinning in circles. Gradually, our steps fell in with a six-eight beat. The Dragon lifted his right hand and placed it on my hip as if to escort me. He squeezed my right hand with his left, and we were in proper dance position.

Gazing into one another's eyes, we danced on. Before I realized what was happening, my feet floated off the ballroom floor. We rose into the air like we were circling an invisible staircase until we reached the crumbling dome overhead. My heart pounded with excitement and a smile spread over my face. The Dragon gazed at me with wide eyes.

I noticed the mermaids looking up at us. They were smiling, which loosened the knot of tension in my chest a tiny bit. The mermaids were completely devoted to the Dragon. I wanted them to see me as more than a nuisance.

Points of light flew around the castle dome, and from them, a single beam shot up like a comet. The comet was the Dragon and me. We spun round and round like a satellite, clinging to each other as we soared through a sky full of stars.

It's not so hard living all by yourself
It isn't hard, yes; I know that's what you'll say
It's what you have told yourself over and over again in darkness
You try to hold back all the thoughts

But you know,
I just want you as you are
Just the you that I see right before me
It's all that has been on my mind

Lend me your voice
Let me see your face, let me start
to show you what I see
Bring me close
Let me feel the beat of your heart,
the secret you bury

Lend me your voice!
Anything you want to say,
I'll be right here, I'll listen; so tell me
Open the door
Let me come and sit by the fire,
just let me come close to your heart

I gazed at the Dragon as we danced.

He didn't take his eyes off me, although they were clouded with embarrassment. He had spent his life fighting. It seemed he was experiencing everything else for the first time.

As that thought occurred to me, I felt an almost painful tenderness rise within me. Letting my feelings guide me, I placed my hand on his jaw and very slowly brought my face toward his. Closing my eyes, I lifted my mouth to him.

I felt him tense up, then close his eyes tight.

Maybe it was too soon.

I smiled and lay my cheek against him. My first kiss would have to wait. He reached out his hand apologetically, drew me gently to him, and slowly closed his eyes.

Afterward, we returned to the castle. On the dark balcony beneath the starry heavens, we nestled together. The Dragon slept defenselessly against my chest.

I don't know how much time passed like that. Suddenly, I heard what sounded like a ceramic dish breaking in the distance. The Dragon's eyelids flew open, and he let out a wounded howl.

"What's the matter?" I asked, but he didn't answer. He pressed his hand against his face, got to his feet, and began walking away, shaking. But then, perhaps no longer able to stand it, he sank to his knees and hunched over the ground.

I saw something that made me doubt my eyes.

The bruises on the Dragon's back were quivering. It was as if he was being beaten by an invisible hand. He started grunting horribly as a way to withstand the pain.

"Ungh... Ngh... Ngh...!"

I didn't know what to make of it.

"What's happening…?"

"Don't...look at me...!!"

He turned slightly toward me and looked at me with tormented eyes.

The angel AS was lounging on the balcony floor, watching like this was an everyday occurrence.

"Who…are you?" I whispered to the Dragon.

He didn't answer.

Overhead, a million stars twinkled.

ON EDGE

A soft rain was falling outside the classroom windows.

Hiro sat with her chin in her hand, scrolling down as she read U comments out loud to me.

"'Belle's not doing any more concerts?'

"'I want to hear Belle sing again.'

"'Why won't she sing anymore?'

"'Must be scared another concert will get interrupted.'

"'It's all the Dragon's fault.'

"'Wish they'd unveil him already.'"

I sat with my feet on my chair and my arms around my knees, listening to what people were writing. All of them hurt.

"Let's forget about the Dragon. We don't need to know his secrets," I said.

"It doesn't matter anymore. U isn't some little class group chat. No one can stop it now."

Hiro switched to an anonymous message board.

GTFO Beast

Worthless scum

He can die for all I care.

It was a solid stream of merciless, unthinking hatred.

My phone lay on my desk with a video by the Justices playing on it.

"The dangerous Beast is threatening order in U. We are seeking new information about him via the hashtag #UnveilTheBeast."

I felt like he was being hounded from all directions.

A bearded man was watching some AS streamer making a fuss.

"He's just some stupid old hermit!"

A girl in glasses was seated on a park bench, watching another AS offer a rebuttal:

"He's a genius kid gamer!"

A middle schooler had her phone under her desk and was secretly watching a livestream where an AS whispered, "The Beast is actually a mind-blowingly hot chick."

A guy in a rugby shirt was leaning on a locker room wall, watching a different stream.

"I heard he's a billionaire."

An elderly woman and her daughter were at home, watching a livestream on the sofa.

"I'm suing him for the emotional trauma I suffered from fighting him."

A woman was viewing a gossip video where a reporter confronted Jelinek and his new girlfriend.

"Dating already, are you? I thought the love of your life just died," the reporter said.

His girlfriend, a plump, dark-skinned woman with curly blond hair, spoke to the waiting mics.

"He's incredible."

In another video, his pale, black-haired ex was protesting, her glasses flashing.

"Hey, I'm not dead!"

"She's still alive?" his current girlfriend asked, surprised.

Jelinek defended himself from a separate window.

"I never said *she* was the one who died."

But his ex was exploding with rage. "He's such a fake! He copied the Beast's bruises for all his tattoos."

"She's lying!" Jelinek insisted, pressing his hand to his forehead.

"He's a total fraud!"

"Bitter losers like you should just keep their mouths shut," his new girlfriend said with a shrug.

"What did you call me?!"

Jelinek blocked the camera, his patience gone. "How dare you claim I'm a fraud!"

Fox, the outfielder for the Wildebeests, wasn't the type to get easily ruffled, so he said nothing. He just kept smiling at his fans, trying to be a good person. He didn't let occasional criticism put him out of sorts or throw him off. He didn't subscribe to the belief that baseball was all about racking up good stats. To the contrary, he thought the better his stats, the humbler he should be. Nothing was accomplished alone. The only reason he was here was because of his teammates, fans, opponents, and all the people who loved baseball.

Still, this time, he felt he couldn't overlook the gossip, or rather the nastiness that was being directed at him. He earnestly believed he needed to communicate his true intentions. The problem was finding the right way to get those intentions across.

In the end, he chose to create a video message.

Having decided to broadcast from his low-key home study, he set up his camera on a tripod and pressed the livestream button.

Dressed in a high-necked undershirt, he took off his team cap and set it on the side table before quietly beginning to speak.

"People think I'm hiding something because I don't show my skin in public. Lately, some have even been saying that I'm the Beast on U. But I'm no villain, and I'm not violent. I want to be a true hero for children."

Fox stood slowly and took off his undershirt. The skin of his upper body, the skin he'd kept so closely guarded, was exposed to the camera. Long scars covered his torso. One stretched from beneath his neck to the center of his chest. Another traversed his right side, another crossed above his stomach, and another was over its center. The right side of his torso was dotted with marks where drains had been inserted. He truly was scarred from head to toe.

"Please don't be shocked. I was seriously ill as a child and required many major surgeries. But it's thanks to those operations that I'm healthy enough to play baseball," he said calmly. He placed his hand on his chest.

"To all the kids watching this: Don't give up on your dreams. I hope this message comes across the right way."

Fox's livestream was playing on multiple large screens in U. Although viewers were shocked by the vivid scars, his honesty earned him overwhelmingly positive comments. The ASes of U cheered his gentlemanly performance.

Hiro's AS was watching with her arms crossed.

"Interesting..."

Fox had been one of her suspects, and now that her guess turned out to be wrong, she was at a loss.

"So who *is* the Dragon?"

His mermaid attendants were sleeping. Ever since our dance at the castle, Hiro's AS had been looking after them like a big sister.

Suddenly, someone shouted, "Inexcusable!"

Hiro turned, recognizing the voice.

"Oh, wow..."

An ad was playing on a floating screen. The phrase "You hurt me" was written in various languages. Hiro walked closer on a hunch. A baby was screaming hysterically in the foreground, clutching a teddy bear.

"I won't take it! I'll never forgive the people who hurt me! Never!"

"Are you...the ideal housewife lady?" Hiro's AS asked.

"Huh?"

The baby—that is, Swan—looked up in surprise at having been identified.

"Why are you a baby?" Hiro's AS pressed.

"The true me is innocent at heart!"

"That's a lie. I bet you think you can get away with saying whatever awful things you want as long as you have a cute avatar."

The baby AS responded to this merciless accusation with a wail.

"Wahhh...! Shut up!!"

She abruptly hurled the teddy bear.

"Ack!" Hiro's AS yelped, flinching.

The baby AS took the opportunity to crawl away at top speed. Hiro's AS slumped her shoulders. Another of her suspects had just been ruled out.

In central U, large screens crowded the street, Times Square style. They were displaying various images of Belle—I mean, of me. The AS spectators spewed countless comment bubbles:

Is Belle really going to sing again?

That's just a rumor
I heard she's gonna hold a surprise concert.
There's nothing to back that up.
But if it's true...

I didn't plan to sing yet. But everyone was so full of expectations and disappointment and hope. I didn't know how to respond. All I could do was hide my bewildered face behind my scarf.

"......?!"

Sensing a presence nearby, I turned.

I was surrounded by high-level Justices. They'd seized on a brief moment when I was away from Hiro's AS and the mermaids.

I was brought in for interrogation immediately. They hung up my scarf and cloak and sat me down in a wooden chair. Other than a circle of marble flooring illuminated by a light hanging from the ceiling, my surroundings were dark. I felt like I was on a stage.

Justin was wearing a black suit and tie. He held out the insignia on his right arm to show me.

"Do you know why this light has the power of justice?"

I said nothing. He pulled back the insignia.

"Normally, biometric information scanned by devices is converted into the registered AS using a special process. This light blocks the conversion. As a result, the AS's origin is projected here in U. That's how unveiling works. I essentially possess the same power held exclusively by the Voices, this world's creators."

"_____"

"Have you ever wondered why there are no police on the internet? It's odd, isn't it, that U has no law enforcement? That's what everyone thinks, and for good reason. But the Voices ignore the issue, insisting that U already has everything necessary for a fair and equal society."

Justin gazed into the distance with a look of righteous indignation.

"We disagree. Bad actors exist everywhere. There are criminal elements who harass the public and seed chaos, people who do as they please and thumb their noses at the world. The good guys need the power to resist these bad actors. Justice is necessary everywhere. Forces of good are needed to knock down evil. We are that force."

He punched his palm passionately.

"That Beast—that hideous Dragon is exactly the kind of creature that must be unveiled to maintain U as we know it. So—"

He turned slowly toward me.

"—why are you always with him?" he asked.

"Why…?" I repeated.

Pinned to my chest was the pale pink rose the mermaids had given me on that night with the Dragon. I stared at it. Justin looked down at me expressionlessly.

"Tell me where the Beast is. Make no mistake—you won't get away with remaining silent. So start talking. This instant. Or—"

His right hand transformed into a lion's head. He turned it toward me.

"Or shall I unveil you here and now?"

I hesitated but felt none of the panic that had overwhelmed me before.

"…I wouldn't tell you even if I did know," I replied.

"What?!"

I looked up at him and said quietly, "You have nothing to do with justice. You just want to force people into submission. That's why I won't tell you anything."

"……!!"

Justin's outrage abruptly surfaced. His huge hand grabbed my head violently. I gasped. The coatrack crashed to the ground. Like a gun being cocked, the lens emerged from the lion's head. The wooden chair toppled over. A petal fell from the rose on my chest as it shook.

Justin thrust the lens in front of my head, which was still grasped in his hand, and threatened me in a voice seething with anger. The lens began to shine.

"I refuse to continue letting you make a fool of me. You think I can't unveil you? Fine. Let's test that theory."

I struggled in vain to escape, pressed down by his powerful arms.

"Who is the songstress the world loves so much? What sort of face hides beneath her beautiful skin? I have a few guesses. And besides…"

My heart pounded in my ears.

"…I doubt anyone will take your music seriously once the truth comes out."

Justin smiled brutally, as if he were reveling in the experience of hurting me.

"If you want to avoid that fate, then tell me: Who is the Beast? Where is he now?"

I couldn't escape. Maybe he had won.

Just as I was about to lose hope, I heard a familiar voice.

"Looking for something?"

"Hmm?"

Justin glanced in the direction of the voice. What I had thought was a dark room was now a sunny white beach.

"What's this?!" Justin shouted.

"I'll tell you, but only you. Don't tell anyone else."

It was the mermaids. They were floating alluringly in a circle next to an oasis where blue water bubbled, giggling and laughing.

"Ngh..."

Clearly shaken by this strange development, Justin tried chasing them off by bellowing, "Begone, you pests!!"

The mermaids scattered like minnows. At the same time, an enormous flame roared upward.

"Argh!!"

Justin looked up in a daze. The flame brushed the ceiling, swirling like a whirlpool. Then, in the blink of an eye, the scorching fire turned into a fountain of water. Streams beat down on Justin like waterfalls.

"Goddamn it!!"

He was completely soaked, at the water's mercy. I looked up. Between the cascades, I saw a mermaid with a kerchief tied under her chin.

"Oh!"

When our eyes met, she flitted off in a fluster.

Justin fixed his gaze on the mermaid, stepped toward her, and punched her with all his might.

"Eek!!"

The little creature went flying helplessly. The fountain vanished without a trace.

Justin glanced around, panting. Belle was gone. All that remained was the circle of marble floor. Justin examined his surroundings as if he had just woken from a dream and was still shaking the haze from his mind.

Next to the toppled chair, a single pale pink rose petal lay on the floor. He pinched it between his fingers. When he tilted it, the digital data became momentarily translucent.

"……"

He grinned deviously.

I ran after Hiro's AS toward a park on the Main Stream.

"Thank you for saving me!" I said to the mermaids.

They nodded, then returned to looking after their companion who had fainted after being punched by Justin.

"I'm so relieved they found you," Hiro's AS said. But I didn't share her relief. I knew now that the Dragon was in greater danger than ever.

After sunset, I sat in the garden with my arms around my jean-clad knees, watching Fugue eat his dinner. But my mind was on the Dragon.

"He's in danger. I have to be there for him… I have to protect him…"

"Suzu?"

"…Huh?!" I said, jumping up.

It was Dad. I hadn't even noticed he was back from work. I hunched over and said warily, "…What?"

"If anything's bothering you—"

"I'm fine."

"—please just tell me. Anything at all—"

"*Nothing* is wrong!!"

I ran into the house, racing through the living room and up the stairs. Safely in my room, I slammed the door.

"……"

I tried imagining how Dad must feel. He must hate his selfish daughter.

Later, when I went downstairs, the paper bag he'd been holding was in the kitchen. Inside were ripe, fragrant peaches. There was a note next to the bag.

The guys at work gave me these. Help yourself. Dad

The green of summer was glistening all around. I could hear the choir ladies from the old elementary school's gym.

"There aren't many people left here. This village is going to disappear, that's for certain. No one will see the beauty of the mountains or the glitter of the streams anymore. It seems every place other than the big cities is experiencing the same trends. Our village may offer a glimpse of Japan's future."

A group of visitors had come from a shrinking community outside the prefecture to hear what our villagers had to say. About half were women.

"People often ask me why I live in a place like this," Ms. Kita said calmly.

"The city is so much more convenient, they say. And they're right," added Ms. Hatanaka.

"So why do we stay here all the same?" Ms. Okumoto asked, one hand on her hip.

Propped on the upright piano was a framed photo of the choir taken over a decade ago. Six-year-old me was in it, and so was Mom.

"There's still one child here," Ms. Nakai said, as if she'd just remembered. "She's been with us since she was little. She's like our own daughter. For her sake, I want to slow the disappearance of our home, even a little. I'll keep trying until she spreads her wings."

The audience listened intently. Ms. Yoshitani giggled like she was trying to lighten the mood.

"Sorry for the long prelude. We hope you enjoy this song."

The other members smiled at the audience and arranged their sheet music. The gym echoed with their voices. Their smiles in that photo from ten years ago were so beautiful. And they were still just as beautiful.

TINY LOVE

The train pulled out of Ino Station headed for Susaki, its diesel engine chugging. I showed the stationmaster my commuter ticket and walked through the ticket gate, headed home from school. A girl sitting on a bench in the waiting room saw me and stood up.

"Hi, Suzu."

I turned around.

"Ruka?"

What's she doing here?

She looked upset and very anxious to talk to me. Her alto sax was over her shoulder, but it was too early for practice to be over. Whatever she wanted to talk about must be important enough for her to skip band.

We got on the bus and sat next to each other as it bumped along the mountain road. Ruka said the contrast of the blue Niyodo River and the white banks was pretty. I appreciated her kind words, but I knew she hadn't come here to sightsee. She must've been having a hard time bringing up the real reason.

We got off at my bus stop and crossed the Chinka Bridge. The shadows of clouds drifted over the mountains.

"I struck out," she suddenly said.

"You what?"

"Your text gave me the courage to shoot my shot."

"Uh-huh?"

"But once I was with him, I couldn't bring myself to say it."

"Ah."

"And then he said, 'Why are you acting like that? You're creeping me out.'"

Ruka stopped in the middle of the bridge.

"What the heck?! That's awful!" I shouted.

"No, I deserved it. I have zero confidence. And I really *was* being creepy…"

She smiled and shook her head, but she was looking down at the ground and had her eyes squeezed shut. How could he say a thing like that to such a pretty girl?

"That's not true!" I insisted. "You didn't deserve that! Shinobu's such a jerk!"

She looked up with a start and waved her hands in protest. "What? No, not him."

"Huh? Then…?"

She looked down again and muttered, like the words were hard to get out, "…It was Chikami."

"Who's Chikami?"

She glanced around nervously before finally managing to say, "Shinjiro…Chikami."

"Kamishin?!"

Ruka closed her eyes and nodded.

When we got home, I made a snack in the kitchen: slices of chilled peaches in iced tea. Ruka was in the yard, scratching Fugue's head and chin. She had her face right up next to his. I guess she wasn't put off by his missing paw.

"You're so cute!" she cooed. Fugue wagged his tail and licked Ruka's cheek.

She and I sat on the veranda and drank peach tea. The ice made a refreshing *clink* in my mug.

"This is delicious," she said.

"Oh, I'm glad."

Fugue was sitting with his tail up against Ruka's feet. He seemed to like her.

Ruka shot me a sidelong glance, setting down her glass. "I figured out who you like now."

I waved my hands in a panic. "Don't say it! I'll die of embarrassment!"

"Okay. So how long have you liked him?" she asked, peering at me.

I looked up at the sky, trying to remember. Thunderheads were gathering.

"When I was six years old, he promised to protect me. At first, I thought he was proposing to me. But what he really meant was that he'd protect me from bullies. He wasn't proposing at all."

She didn't respond.

"After my mom died, I used to cry all the time. It scared the other kids in class, so they kept their distance. He must have thought they were bullying me..."

I took a sip of iced tea from my chipped mug. Ruka watched me until I put it down, then she smiled and turned away as if to change the subject.

"This might sound weird, but I've always thought he acted a bit like your mom."

"My mom?"

"I mean, he's always asking you if you're okay, even when nothing's happened, right? Shinobu's not like other guys..."

Realizing what she just said, she brought one long finger to her cheek.

"Oops, I said it." She giggled.

I did, too. "And now I'm dead."

We laughed together.

We took the bus back along the Niyodo River and got off at Ino Station, still talking as we entered the building. A train bound for Kochi Station was waiting.

When she got to the ticket gate, Ruka looked back at me.

"You should take me to the elementary school where you guys met one of these days."

"Okay."

"I'll come again."

"Right."

I smiled back at her. She glanced at the corner of the waiting room and let out a little yelp. I followed her gaze. A boy was sitting at the end of the bench, staring at his phone.

"...Kamishin?"

"Oh, hey."

He looked up at me but remained seated. Ruka stood rooted to the ground, staring at him. Kamishin also kept looking at us, unmoving. An awkward minute passed. The train and bus both left, like they were tired of waiting. I looked back and forth between Ruka and Kamishin, on opposite sides of the room.

I have to say something. I have to break the deadlock—!

"H-hey, guys, let's go somewhere over summer break. Ruka, where do you want to go? Kamishin, know any good places?"

"I'm out," he answered.

"What?"

"Championships."

"Oh, right. I remember now. We'll go watch the game. Where is it? We can get there."

"Hokkaido."

"...Um, that's way too far."

"Not my fault."

"Can't they do it any closer?"

"Don't be dumb."

"I—I—I...," Ruka suddenly said. "I—I—I'll root for you."

"...Huh? Root?"

"At th-the championships...," she said so softly I could hardly hear.

The word "root" seemed to trigger something in Kamishin. He stood up, holding his sports bag.

"You'll root for me...?"

"Kamishin."

"Hey, Suzu?"

"What?"

"She said she's gonna root for me."

"Yeah."

"Does that mean—*ahem*—that she likes me a little?"

Ruka's school bag fell from her hand with a *thud*.

"Just kidding, just kidding!" Kamishin said, like he'd been waiting to say that. He smiled awkwardly, both hands up in protest. Ruka was looking down silently and covering her bright red face.

"...What?" Kamishin asked me, sounding confused. I nodded dramatically.

"Huh...?" He still didn't get it, so he looked at me again. I nodded once more, this time *very* dramatically.

When it finally clicked for him, he exclaimed, "Whaaaaat?!" and almost fell over.

For a moment, nobody moved. Then, still on the verge of collapsing, he nimbly backed out of the station.

"Hey, wait!!" I yelled, running after him.

When I caught up to him outside, he was freaking out.

"Why are you running away?" I asked.

"No one's ever said they liked me!"

"Well, you heard her, didn't you? About how she'll root for you?"

"...Oh."

"Aren't you happy?"

"...Yeah."

"Then you should reciprocate."

"...Right."

Kamishin toddled back to Ruka.

"I...uh..."

His expression tense, he attempted to talk to her even as she covered her face with her hands.

"Ahhhhh!!"

But then—still nearly bent over backward—he nimbly retreated from the station yet again.

"Wait!!" I yelled, running after him.

I caught up to him outside. He was even more freaked out than before.

"I dunno how to talk to girls!"

"Just say whatever. Like thanks or I'll do my best."

"...Oh."

"Now go say it."

"...Uh-huh."

After a minute, he walked awkwardly over to her and stood there, still bent slightly backward.

No one said anything.

"W-Watanabe," he finally said to Ruka, who was covering her face.

"...Yes?" she said, lowering her hands.

"Um...what sort of things are you into?"

"...Music," she replied, pointing to her sax case. "What kind of music do you like?"

"B-Belle, and stuff like that."

"?!"

I nearly jumped at this unexpected development.

Ruka's face suddenly brightened. "Oh! I listen to Belle all the time!"

Kamishin smiled. "For real? Same here."

"I so wish I could sing like her... Don't laugh, but people tell me we look alike."

"?!?!?!"

I teetered back in shock.

"You totally do," Kamishin said.

"You must think I'm full of myself."

"No way, you guys are seriously twins. Wait, are you related? You gotta be," he said, straight-faced. Ruka attempted to cool her flaming cheek with the back of her hand.

"...I'm so embarrassed."

I backed slowly out of the station, hoping they wouldn't notice. Kamishin was talking like his usual self now. Ruka seemed more relaxed, too.

"My grandfather works at a shipyard in Hakodate, and we always go there in the summer. So, um...if it's okay with you, I can cheer you on at the championships."

"F-for real? I'll definitely crush it if you come. Just watch me."

"...Okay."

I was through the turnstile and out to the intersection. I looked back at the station, pressing my hand to my chest.

That was close...

I let out a sigh of relief. Whenever I heard Belle mentioned in public, my heart would start beating and I'd get the urge to run and hide. It was even worse when Ruka and Kamishin talked about her.

I hope it works out for them...

Things seemed to be going swimmingly after her little confession. I had high hopes for those two. As long as no one interrupted...

"Suzu!"

I looked back toward the intersection. The light was red; Shinobu was across the street outside the convenience store, staring at me.

"...Oh."

"Did you see Kamishin?"

I glanced back at the station. I could see the two of them talking.

"Ye...no," I said, changing my nod to a head shake.

"Which is it?"

"Mm... Mm-mm."

I really wanted him to leave them alone in this crucial moment.

Several cars passed loudly between us. My hair and clothes fluttered in the dusty wind.

Shinobu changed the subject. "Suzu...there's something I've been wanting to tell you for a long time."

"There is?"

"I..."

I could tell he was trying to say something important.

"Oh!" I spluttered, imagining what it might be.

Is it...? No, no way. But maybe? No, definitely not. But still... Still...

I started blushing. Was this the right time? Would I be able to say what I'd been wanting to?

"S-sorry, Shinobu! There's something I've been wanting to tell you, too."

"...Okay."

"Actually, I—"

"I know."

"I'm—"

"You're Belle, right?"

"What?"

I froze.

"Belle is you, right?" he shouted at me across the road.

My whole body was quivering from shock. I felt like the ground was crumbling under my feet.

"Ahhhhhh!" I screamed.

"Suzu."

Two or three cars passed between us. My hair and clothes fluttered again.

"You're wr-wr-wrong!!" I shouted.

"Suzu."

"No!!" I shrieked.

Another string of cars drove by. A gust of wind blew, and Shinobu squinted. By the time all the cars had passed, I was gone. He looked around for me.

"Suzu? Suzu, where'd you go?"

I ran all the way to the bank of the Niyodo. I was panting hard, totally shaken up. My legs trembling and weak, I sank to my knees, gripped my head, and shook it back and forth.

"Ahhhhhh!"

What was going on? How did Shinobu know? Here I was trying so desperately to keep it secret, and the one person I least wanted to know had found out. How mortifying. It was over. Everything was over. Despair overwhelmed me.

"Aaargh, what do I do? I can never let him see me again..."

I covered my face with my hands and sobbed. That was all I could do. Just then, my phone rang.

"Huh?!"

When I answered, I heard Hiro's frantic voice on the other end:

"Suzu!! The Dragon's in trouble!!"

TRUE SELVES

The Justices gathered in the ruined unit. After they passed through the gate separating the park district from the skyscraper district, the Hidden Pool Waterfall, Primeval Wood of Mystery, and Flat Shallow Coast flashed by in seconds, segueing into a sea of clouds. Normally the clouds functioned to keep strangers out, but the Justices passed through instantaneously, like they had some special passcode.

The clouds cleared to reveal the Dragon's castle.

But instead of the closed space it had been up till now, it was an ordinary space like U's Main Stream. The castle was clearly visible from every angle.

The Dragon's castle...

Has finally...

Been exposed

ASes watched anxiously to see what would happen.

The Justices broke down the castle doors with a crash and flooded in.

"Yaaaaaah!" they roared.

The broad entrance hall was instantly filled with troops. They pushed and shoved up the staircase carrying hammers, chains, and drills, then ran headlong down the hallway. Chaotic destruction reigned in every corner of the castle.

The courtyard was no exception. The troops busted in with their shoes on and trampled the rose garden. The pink and black rosebushes were mercilessly ripped from the ground, torn to pieces, trampled underfoot.

Justin delivered a message to all the ASes in U:

"We will not back down! The Beast's origin will be brought to light!!"

In between his fingers was the rose petal he'd picked up while interrogating Belle. He had determined the location of the Dragon's castle by analyzing data in the petal.

"He will pay for his sins before all of U!!"

A phalanx of corporate logos emerged behind Justin as he spoke. The Justices had more corporate sponsors than ever before.

"Heh..."

Justin turned to count the logos with a satisfied smile.

The Beast will finally be unveiled!

ASes thronged the streets, watching the drama unfold. On the huge screens lining U's Main Stream, a live broadcast from the Dragon's castle played alongside larger-than-life images of the Dragon himself overlaid with the words "WHO IS THE BEAST?"

I wonder who he really is

Everyone wants to know.

They say he's some psycho killer still on the loose.

I heard he's a corrupt tax-evading businessman

The Dragon's image was quickly blotted out by thoughtlessly cruel comment bubbles.

Get lost, Beast!

You're worthless.
He might as well just disappear

Mr. Reseggnation and Hey-o Doggo were livestreaming the castle situation on their YouTube channel.

"Hey, Dragon!" Mr. Reseggnation screamed. "You watching this?! Huh?!"

"I doubt it," Hey-o Doggo said, ever the rational one.

"Kids around the world are on your side! Are you watching? Are ya?!"

"I told you, he's not. Unfortunately."

Hey-o Doggo started reading out the names of children from around the world who had sent messages.

"Here's Ian, age thirteen, Harper, age fourteen, and Amelia, age twelve."

"Grown-ups are bullying the Dragon!"

They were calling in their complaints from their phones.

"You listening, Dragon?!"

"Next we have Oliver, age eleven, Liam, age ten, Emma, age nine, and Aida, age ten."

"I feel bad for him!"

"You're good people, kids. So sweet."

"Next are a couple of our regulars: Camille, age sixteen, and Jake, age thirteen."

"Somebody save him!"

"Thanks for all your comments, guys! Keep it up!"

"Now let's hear from Jiali, age thirteen, Yiran, age twelve, Junjie, age thirteen, and Haoran, age twelve."

"We need to cheer him on!"

"Hear that, Dragon? You're one lucky dude!"

"Next we've got Charlie, age eighteen, Leo, age nine, and their friend."

"There's still time."

"Yeah, it's not too late."

"Next is Tomo, age eleven. I recognize that name."

"L-let's support...the Dragon..."

"Anything from Kei, age fourteen?" Hey-o Doggo asked, but Tomo ignored him and kept talking.

"W-we should all...cheer him on..."

Suddenly, someone else burst into the feed with Mr. Reseggnation and Hey-o Doggo.

"Agh!"

"Get real, loser!" The pudgy young intruder, who was wearing goggles, pointed mockingly at Tomo's viewer number. *"You've got, like, three viewers!"*

Mr. Reseggnation and Hey-o Doggo protested.

"An intruder! Where'd he come from?! This is awful!"

"Who are you?! Go away!"

Other young people started laughing at the viewer numbers in Tomo and Kei's video chat.

"No one cares!!"

"The Dragon can go to hell!"

"Screw the Dragon!"

"Quit that! This is our stream!"

"Get out! Darn it! Stop!"

More teenagers laughed at the desperation of the two boys.

"They're trying way too hard!!"

"Bite me, Dragon!"

"Get bent!"

"Enough already! You're so mean! Stop!"

"Jerks! You're all idiots! Get outta here!"

Mr. Reseggnation and Hey-o Doggo dropkicked the invaders' chat windows over and over.

"......!!"

I jumped up in shock. Hiro was yelling at me over the phone.

"Meet me at the old school!"

"Got it!"

Forgetting all my worries from just moments ago, I took off running down the riverbank. As I ran, I pushed my earbuds into my ears. The devices pinged. The U app started up on my phone. The body-sharing began.

I put my hand on the door to U and shoved it open.

The Dragon's castle towered before my eyes, smoke curling from different parts of it. I climbed over the splintered door. Inside the entryway, the carved banister and pillars had been reduced to rubble by the rampaging Justices. I climbed the grand staircase and ran down the hallway. Holes had been punched in the walls, doors were off their hinges, and the glass ceiling was shattered.

When I reached the ballroom, I gasped.

Mermaids littered the floor. They were badly wounded and struggling for breath.

"Oh...!" I ran to them in horror. Kneeling, I lifted the white sea slug mermaid in my arms.

"Why...?"

Who attacked them?

The wounded mermaid looked up at me, her eyes barely open.

"Protect...our master...," she whispered.

Her words touched my heart. Such a tiny thing, and yet she was so worried about the great Dragon. My eyes filled with tears. I wanted to fulfill her wish—but how?

Footsteps thundered through the castle.

"Huh?!"

Justin burst into the ballroom, trailing the other Justice leaders. Crossing his arms menacingly, he gazed down at the battered mermaids.

"They refused to tell us where the Beast is," he said.

"How could you do something so awful?" I pleaded, looking up at him.

"Don't worry about them. They're just AI," he said casually, tilting his head like it was no big deal.

I was so furious I felt like my hair was standing on end. To him, everyone was merely an object to be controlled. Troops ran into the room.

"We can't find him," they informed Justin.

"Then we'll leave."

They quickly filed out the door. Justin looked back at me and said, "Burn the castle down."

I gasped.

"We'll smoke him out like a rat from his hole."

With that, he strode off.

"......!"

I was left behind to bite my lip in helpless desperation. Just then, the pretty white sea slug mermaid signaled to me with her eyes.

"Look...behind...you."

I did as she said. One of the gates was blocked off with stones. I was sure it had been open before; I recognized the spiral pattern above it.

"I will tell…only you," the mermaid said, slowly closing her eyes, as those words had taken her last drop of strength.

A square gap opened in the stone, and it began to recede in pieces split by cracks.

A hidden passage appeared.

I passed through the gate and climbed the crumbling spiral staircase. The pixelation was even worse than before. It seemed on the verge of collapsing. At the top of the stairs, I saw a balcony.

"……!"

The Dragon lay collapsed on the floor.

"No!!" I screamed, running to him.

He struggled to sit up, grasping the balcony banister as he panted and groaned. It didn't seem like the Justices had injured him. Instead, he appeared to be suffering in the same way he had on the night we danced, when he had suddenly hunched his back beneath invisible blows. Was an invisible hand beating him now, too?

"It's all right. Try to calm down," I said, standing beside him. I tugged at the hem of his cape, trying to lead him out of the castle. "It's dangerous here. Escape with me."

But the Dragon only whispered with ragged breath, "Just gotta get through this… I just gotta get through this…" He seemed to be talking to himself.

"…'Gotta'?"

It was strange to hear him say that—like a kid, almost. He looked at me with kind eyes.

"Belle… I'm sorry I never told you the truth…," he whispered, gripping the banister.

"No—wait!!"

Before I could stop him, he jumped over the banister and began to fall.

"Wait!!"

Twisting as he fell, he caught an updraft and soared toward the Main Stream, leaving the ruins of his castle behind. I stared after him helplessly.

As Justin had promised, flames licked up from the Dragon's castle. Fire engulfed the building within moments. The photograph over the fireplace in the Dragon's room burned with everything else, the flames obscuring the woman behind the cracked glass.

In minutes, everything was burned to the ground, as if the entire castle had been made of paper.

Kamishin and Ruka were sitting side by side in the Ino Station waiting area, looking at their phones, when Shinobu came in.

"Hey, Shinobu, look at this. Everything's going to hell in U," Kamishin said, holding out his phone.

An online newscast was broadcasting footage of the burning castle. The scene cut to an image of Belle searching for something. The chyron read, "Belle appears." Shinobu stared at it.

"...Suzu."

"Suzu?"

"Do you guys know where she went?"

"I dunno..."

"Earlier Suzu was telling me about her elementary school," said Ruka. "Is that anywhere near here?"

"......!"

Shinobu's head jerked up like a puzzle piece had just fallen into place. He glanced around and ran out of the station.

"H-hey, Shinobu!" Kamishin shouted in confusion. Ruka ignored him and took off jogging, too.

"Huh? ...Ruka!!"

Kamishin gave up and followed.

Around the same time, I was arriving at the classroom in the old school.

"Suzu! What took you so long?!" Hiro hollered.

"Sorry!"

"I'm running an autosearch of pages that might be relevant," she said. On the large monitor, windows were popping up all over a world map.

"We have to figure out who he is before the Justices capture him!"

"How?" Hiro demanded. "He could be in another country. He could be on the other side of the world. We'll never find one person out of five billion accounts!"

"Where is he?! Where did he go?!"

I searched for him among the countless glittering buildings of U's bustling streets. But this world was so big, and there were so many ASes.

The ASes, meanwhile, didn't have a hard time finding me.

"Look, it's Belle!"

"Belle?!"

"Belle!!"

They peeked between their fingers and pushed aside their hair to look. All sorts of ASes were staring at me in shock.

"It's Belle!"

"Is it really her?"

"She came back to us after all!"

A crowd rapidly gathered around me.

"Talk about a rare sighting!"

"Sing for us!"

"Sing!!"

"Stop! I have to find him!" I pleaded, trying to push forward, but a horde of ASes was hemming me in.

"Let me through! Please!!"

I swam, panting, among the sea of ASes. But they surged like a huge wave, and soon only my head was free.

"No…!!"

They flocked around me in a massive clump.

"She's finally gonna sing again!"

"She really is doing a surprise show!"

"I've been waiting for this, Belle!"

"I'm dying to hear your voice!"

"Sing!!"

Hiro watched in a daze as I was swallowed up.

"Everyone, let her go!! We're in a hurry!" she begged, but no one listened.

More and more ASes eager to hear Belle sing were sucked into the ever-growing mass.

"She's surrounded," Ms. Okumoto said, pausing to look at her phone as she weeded her garden.

"This looks bad," Ms. Hatanaka murmured, standing at her university lectern after a class ended.

"But if we go to her…" Ms. Kita was in an apron, resting her elbows on the bar of the izakaya where she worked.

"Then she'll realize we knew all along," said Ms. Nakai, wearing a white coat. She had just finished seeing her last patient of the day.

"But still…," Ms. Yoshitani began, dressed in waders as she peeled off her rubber gloves at the wharf. "I think we should go."

Inside the windows of their group chat, all the members of the choir started getting ready.

Hiro was screaming at the ASes on the big screen.

"Please, everyone!! Let her through!"

I stood quietly next to her, my hands on my chest and my eyes closed. I was trying to think back over everything I knew and find within it his true identity.

"*I've been hurt!*" Swan had screamed, her eyes sharp. In that video chat, she was smiling brightly. Behind these polarized images was a third where a sobbing baby AS symbolized her lonely heart.

Was the Dragon, like her, isolated somewhere?

"*I got my tattoos in the same places the love of my life was injured,*" Jelinek had said in response to an interviewer's question. On his website were pictures of him showing the swollen tattoos on his pale skin. But I was sure the Dragon's bruises weren't put there by design.

"*I was seriously ill as a child and required many major surgeries,*" Fox the baseball player had confessed. But somehow, the Dragon's bruises were different from those very real surgical scars.

U devices picked up inflammatory reactions in the wearer's body. When I hit my forehead, Belle got a red mark on her forehead. Maybe the same bruises existed on the back of the real person behind the Dragon.

As I thought about it, I remembered that when I felt emotional pain, a round, bruise-like mark appeared on Belle's chest. The round mark gave off a soft, warm light. If emotional pain was transformed into visible marks, was that why the bruises on the Dragon's back quivered so strangely the night we danced…?

And when we clung to each other in the starry sky…

…his eyes had looked just like a child's.

"A child…?"

I gasped.

"La la la…la la…la la la…"

Somewhere in the distance, I heard what sounded like a child humming.

"That's a child's voice!"

It was coming from one of the countless windows open on the screen.

"La la la…la la…la la la…"

"He and I are the only ones who know that song!"

It was the melody I had written, the song Belle had sung in the ballroom. I was certain.

"Where's it coming from?!"

I searched the screen frantically.

Shinobu, Kamishin, and Ruka had just shown up and were watching from the back of the room.

"Suzu…," Ruka whispered worriedly.

I desperately moved the mouse, sorting through the endless windows from Hiro's automated search.

"Where is he? Where?!"

Windows flew away in all four directions.

"La la la…la la…la la la…"

The singing was getting closer.

Finally, I arrived at a single window. A boy wearing a white hoodie was staring out from a white room, singing.

"La la la…la la…la la la…"

It was a live feed. In the corner of the screen, a message read, LIVE: 1 VIEWER. In other words, I was the only one watching.

"......!!"

I stared in surprise. I recognized the boy sitting there singing with hollow eyes.

"I've seen him somewhere..."

I quickly remembered—he was on Mr. Reseggnation's YouTube channel:

"The Dragon...is...my hero."

He'd seemed somehow different from the other kids. In that one related video, he had been with his father and older brother.

"We're a happy little family of three. We're doing just fine without Mom around. We support each other."

"Why is this kid singing my song...?"

Why was he humming the melody I'd danced to with the Dragon?

"I'm gonna enlarge this," Hiro said, starting up a photo-editing app. The boy's face grew larger and larger on the screen. As the image repeatedly became grainy and then cleared up, I made out someone's reflection in his dark, lifeless eyes.

I stared in shock. The person in his eyes was Belle, smiling as she danced with the Dragon in the ballroom.

"Why is she...?"

I blinked, totally stunned. *What do I make of this new information?*

"La la la...la la...la la la..."

The boy strode lightly to the back of his room. It was a big room, but nearly empty. From the angle of the camera, all I could see was the door and one small window. The white wallpaper full of flying birds jumped out at me the most. Pushed up against one wall was a table with a glass vase of red roses on it.

"So is this kid the Dragon?" Hiro asked.

"Something's off," I said.

"Off?"

"I just don't think it's him."

"I agree. I don't see any bruises—," she started saying, when there was a loud *bang* onscreen.

"What was that?!" I shouted, staring at the stream.

The boy's father walked in slowly. I recognized the man from the related video I'd watched before. He'd said he was a single father. He had bushy eyebrows, and he walked confidently, with his chest stuck out. Muscular arms protruded from his shirt sleeves. He wore an expensive-looking silver watch.

"*Tomo, what are you singing?*" he asked quietly.

The boy didn't answer.

"I'm trying to work. You should know how distracting that is."

Tomo ignored him, swaying as he continued to sing. The viewer number in the corner of the screen rose to 2. Someone other than me had started watching.

Tomo kept swaying. His father stared at him.

Suddenly, the man swept the vase off the table with his left hand. It smashed on the floor, the red rose petals scattering like drops of blood. Tomo looked surprised. He stopped humming and slowly plopped down, like a broken puppet.

I stared at the screen in shock, unable to speak. The father raised his thick eyebrows and looked down at Tomo.

"Why don't you ever listen to me?"

The viewer number in the corner of the screen went back to 1. I wondered if the other viewer had retreated out of shock. Hiro and I were the only ones watching now. The boy's father continued.

"The world has rules, and in this house, I make the rules."

Tomo listened to the quiet scolding with a blank expression.

"If you can't obey them, you're nothing to me. How many times do I have to tell you that?"

The man raised his right fist threateningly.

"Because if you still don't get it…"

He was going to hit the boy. I closed my eyes reflexively.

But someone interrupted.

"Stop!!"

A second boy, dressed all in black, stepped between Tomo and the man.

"Leave Tomo alone!!"

He wrestled with their father, managing to hold him back.

"Move."

"Stop it!!"

"Why're you looking at me like that?! I said move!!"

"Ow!!"

The boy in black fell to the ground, and a cracked phone slipped from his pocket. He huddled protectively over Tomo, covering the boy's ears.

"*Tomo, don't listen to him,*" he said.

Their father glared down at them and shouted, "*Who do you have to thank for this roof over your head?!*"

"*It's my fault, not Tomo's,*" the older boy said, his voice barely audible.

"Kei, you're fourteen. You ought to know better by now!"

"It's my fault…"

"What good are you, dammit?!"

Every time his father yelled, Kei's back flinched.

"*It's all my fault,*" he whispered pleadingly, his whole body shaking.

His father kept hurling abuse at him, like some awful boss chastising a subordinate.

"Get out. Do you understand me? If you've got nothing to contribute here, then get out of my sight!!"

With each word, Kei's back trembled like he was being beaten.

"Ungh... Ngh... Ngh...!!"

I remembered how, on the night the Dragon and I spent together, he had trembled and grunted miserably as if he were being beaten by an invisible hand:

"Just gotta get through this... I just gotta get through this..."

The words played in my mind as I watched Kei.

And I realized something else.

The home screen on the phone Kei had dropped—it had a picture of a woman holding a rose. The same photo that had hung in the Dragon's room. The cracks were the same, too—which meant they'd been the cracks in the screen of his phone.

"I found him...," I said out loud.

Between the strands of Kei's disheveled hair, I saw his eyes squeezed shut.

"This boy...is the Dragon."

MASKS

At exactly five o'clock, "The Hazy Moon" began playing over the emergency broadcasting system speakers. The choir members arrived at the old school in rapid succession and parked their cars. They climbed the stairs to the second floor and peeked through the door at the back of the classroom. On the large monitor, a video showed a white room. A faint sound resembling music was coming from the video. Kei was hunched over, stock-still, with his hands covering Tomo's ears. Their father stood looking down on them for a few moments, then turned on his heel and disappeared into the hallway.

There was a loud *bang*, like a door slamming off screen.

"Is that guy really their dad...?" Kamishin muttered.

Ruka stood beside him, speechless. Shinobu watched with a harsh look in his eyes. Onscreen, Tomo was peering worriedly at Kei.

"Kei, are you all right? Kei...?"

Kei stayed where he was, folded limply in half.

I couldn't believe this frail boy was the Dragon.

"Huh... Now it makes sense," Hiro mumbled, half to herself. "Kei wanted to be a hero for Tomo to keep his spirit up. In that case..."

Kei finally lifted his head. Tomo spoke soothingly to him. Hiro watched intently.

"…maybe that's why the Dragon is so strong. If U's body-sharing technology reveals each person's hidden self, then this awful situation must be connected to this boy's strength. Just like how you became Belle, Suzu…"

I wanted to speak directly to Kei. I had to.

I reached for the mouse. There was a chat button in the livestream video—the same feature we'd used to talk with Jelinek and Swan. At the bottom left of the screen, there was a green button to call and a red one to hang up. Pressing the green button would let me talk to him. But I couldn't bring myself to press it.

Would he be able to talk so soon after an experience like that?

The cursor wavered.

Finally, Kei sat up. Tomo stepped away, looking relieved, and sat down with his back against the wall.

It was now or never.

I impulsively gripped the mouse and pressed the green button.

"Now connected," an automated voice said. My (that is, Belle's) chat icon and name appeared on the screen. Kei and Tomo exchanged confused looks. Then they realized what was happening and stared at me. They seemed able to hear me as well.

My heart was pounding in my ears.

"…Can you see me?" I asked, my voice shaking. "Can you hear me? I…saw what happened. Everything…"

Kei gazed at me, then slowly stood. In my eyes, his form blended so perfectly with that of the Dragon. My consciousness shifted naturally to Belle's.

"You're okay now. Everything's going to be fine." I was now

speaking as Belle. "I want to go see you. Can you tell me where you are? Because I—"

But Kei cut me off sharply.

"Who the hell are you?"

"……?!"

He doesn't know…?

Hiro looked up at me in surprise.

"You've never met in person," she said softly.

I went from confused to embarrassed to unsure, but finally stuttered, "I—I'm…Belle."

"…*Belle!*" Tomo said, craning his neck forward.

But Kei only spat, "*You can't be.*"

He was right. Anyone could claim they were Belle. I couldn't prove it. I had no evidence for him. Who would believe the claims of a total stranger?

"Now connected," the automated voice suddenly repeated. Three more chat icons appeared on the screen.

"*See? I told you,*" one of them said.

"Holy crap, this is a crime scene!"

"We've gotta call the police!"

The voices sounded young. One was definitely the person who had entered the room earlier and then left. They'd returned with friends to see what was happening. They barged in, made an irresponsible fuss, then exited the chat, cackling.

The three icons disappeared with a series of clicks, leaving me alone on the screen. The viewer number went back to 1. Kei walked slowly toward the webcam, his expression blank.

"Are you another jerk who wants to laugh at other people's secrets?"

"No, not at all…"

"Did you like what you saw? Was it fun to watch someone suffer?"

"Of course not!!"

He must have thought I was like the three people who had just laughed at him. But I wasn't. Not at all! I desperately held back my tears and kept talking, praying I would somehow get through to him.

"...I want to help you guys. That's why I called. Is there anything I can do to—?"

"*Help? How could you help?*" he interrupted again.

"......!"

How? How could I...?

Kei glared at me.

"Help, help, help. Can't tell you how many times I've heard that before. 'I'll talk to your dad.' 'We spoke with your father. He understands everything now.' But nothing ever changes. Help, help, help. What do you claim you can do?"

I was speechless. I stepped back like a wave of pressure was repelling me.

"Help, help, help. They don't know anything. They say they'll help, but talk is cheap. And they keep on promising to help, help, help. 'We want to help you boys. We want to support you.' Help, help, help. They cry because they pity us. They cry out of sympathy. But in the end, nothing changes."

He kept glaring at me, like he was holding back bottomless anger. Anger at me, but not really at me. Anger at the half-assed ways of the world, at society, at everything. At irresponsible words, heartless attitudes, intolerant minds, unconscious condescension toward the weak, and the deceptions that cover it up. His gaze seemed like a sword aimed at all those things.

"*Help, help, help, help, help, help, help, help, help, help, help! I'm sick of it!!"* he howled, his body shaking like he was spitting out all the anger bottled inside. "*Just leave!!*"

The terrifying look in his eyes was exactly the same look in the Dragon's eyes when he bared his sharp teeth and howled. Like Belle, all I could do was squeeze my eyes shut and shrink into myself.

Kei typed a command on the keyboard. The call ended.

Click.

There was the beeping of a disconnected line, then an error message: An error occurred. Please try again later.

"Kei, answer me!" I cried, pushing the call button frantically. But there was no response.

"He's offline," Hiro muttered. I kept shouting in desperation.

"Where are you?! Tell me!"

"He doesn't trust you!!" Hiro was shouting, too. She looked down and lowered her voice. "He'll never tell you where he is."

"Now what...?" Ruka whispered.

"Yes, what do we do...?" Ms. Kita echoed.

No one had an answer.

Shinobu remained silent. He seemed to be thinking about something. Very deeply, and at great length.

After he was done, he slowly looked up and said, "Sing as your real self."

I gasped like I'd been shot by an arrow.

A voice spoke in the dark.

"Make room for Belle!!"

The crowd of ASes surrounding me stepped back in unison. The space they left was like the inside of a huge egg. Their voices echoed across it.

"Sing for us!"

"Belle!"

"Sing something!"

"Belle!"

"Please!"

"Sing..."

In order to open the inner space, the mass of countless ASes had swelled its outer edge. As I watched, new ASes joined so the mass grew even more enormous. Justin and his fellow top-level Justices gazed on the spectacle from the buildings above.

"Watch closely. If she sings, the Beast will come. It happened before."

He narrowed his eyes, as if training them on his target.

"He'll show up. I'm sure of it!!"

The crowd at the center of the park had grown even bigger. In its midst, I looked down, lost in thought.

Shinobu's voice rang out quietly but firmly in the old classroom.

"Don't talk to him as Belle. Talk to him as Suzu."

I listened, speechless and unmoving.

"Are you crazy, Shinobu?!" Hiro said, glaring at him over her shoulder. "What are you saying?!"

Shinobu ignored her and kept talking, his eyes on me.

"I think that's the only way you'll be able to contact him again."

Hiro leaned over the back of her chair and shouted angrily at him.

"What are you talking about?! Do you even know what that means?! Everything Suzu has worked so hard for will go up in smoke!"

"Argh!!" I moaned, planting both hands on the desk and slumping my shoulders. Hiro was right.

"But it's the only way to gain his trust," Shinobu said, not budging.

Hiro must have decided talking to him was pointless, because she grabbed my arm and started tugging like that would win me over.

"Suzu!! What have you been doing all this for up till now?! Do you want to go back to the unhappy old you?! Back to crying all the time?! Are you okay with that?!"

"Aaaaaaaaaaaargh!! Uuuuuuuuugh!!"

I couldn't even put my agony into words. I just groaned and shook my head over and over.

Ruka and Kamishin had nothing to say.

Ms. Kita was watching the scene with a pained expression.

Ms. Okumoto was looking on tensely. So were Ms. Yoshitani and Ms. Hatanaka.

Ms. Nakai had her arms crossed, a sharp look in her eye.

"The fact is, Tomo and Kei revealed their identities," Shinobu said calmly. "What can you do for them with your mask still on, Suzu? How can you get through to them if you're still hiding your real face?"

I was at a crossroads. What to do?

What to do?

The me in the center of the crowd of ASes was also looking down and shaking my head. Justin seemed to be annoyed by my inaction.

"Rrgh, why won't she sing?!" he barked.

"Hey—!"

Before the other Justices could stop him, he had taken off running.

Justin barged into the crowd and started fighting his way toward the center.

The large monitor in the middle of the classroom showed the scene at the center of the crowd. I stood in front of it, staring down at the floor, thinking.

The window playing the video took up the whole screen. I wavered for a long time. I didn't know what to do.

Then all at once, everything became clear. I knew exactly what I had to do.

I (the real me) made up my mind and slowly lifted my head.

I (the virtual me) made up my mind and slowly lifted my head.

Something was approaching me.

"Sing!!"

It was Justin. He had forced his way through the crowd.

"Call that hideous Beast to you with your music!!"

I gradually raised my left hand, taking him in. Justin thrust out both hands and walked straight toward me.

"Sing!!"

I grabbed his right hand and twisted it.

"Ow!! What are you doing?!"

He looked shaken.

"Shine the light!" I screamed.

"Huh?!"

"Shine the light on me!!"

I stared intently at him. He gazed back at me, wide-eyed with surprise.

A blinding green light suddenly appeared at the center of the crowd. Several bands of light escaped from it, shining outward.

The gathered ASes peered at it curiously.

"What the…?" Justin murmured before howling in shock, "Idiot! Nobody unveils themself!!"

With a loud hum, metal wings shot out of the bracelet on Justin's right arm and began flapping. At the same time, the cannon blasted out its green unveiling light at full strength.

The light engulfed my whole body.

Wind and bubbles and particles of light swirled around me like they were scrubbing me down. My hair, my legs, my arms, my fingers, my nails, my lips—every part of me was torn away.

I remembered what Justin had told me.

"Normally, the biometric information scanned by devices is converted into the registered AS using a special process. This light blocks the conversion. As a result, the AS's origin is projected here in U. That's how unveiling works."

At that very moment, this exact process was unfolding in my own body.

Across U, ASes eager to witness the events that were about to take place flocked to the enormous egg-shaped crowd.

Suddenly, with a deafening *bang*, a crack appeared at the top of the mass. Starting from that point, countless ASes began tumbling downward. Their falls spurred more crumbling of the mass, the cracks spreading like spiderwebs. With a rumble, ASes were swept into the large park district of U's Main Stream. Inside the crumbling mass, someone discovered the small figure emitting the green light. They gasped.

It was Belle. They were sure of it.

Then someone else saw her and screamed.

The screaming soon spread.

"What is that?!"

"What's going on?!"

The ASes were in an uproar. Everyone was pointing and gaping.

As Belle's form faded away inside the halo of green, another brightly sparkling human form slowly descended.

It was a girl in a high school uniform.

A pair of metal wings descended behind her at the same time. Perhaps they broke off after their unveiling duty was complete. The girl descending from the heavens alongside the broken wings looked just like a fallen angel whose wings had been torn off.

That girl was me.

"It's Belle's origin..."

Excitement electrified the crowd as they watched me descend, my identity exposed as the one and only freckled high school kid with her necktie flapping and her pleated skirt flying up in the wind.

"She looks totally different..."

"Except for the freckles."

"Her biometric data is being projected as-is."

Hiro couldn't bear watching.

"Ohhh, I can't take it!!" she cried, covering her face with her hands.

I landed in the egg-shaped space, and the green light blinked off. I could see the crowd of ASes stretching far into the distance. How many millions were there? Tens of millions? Hundreds? I had no idea. I had never seen such an enormous crowd in my life.

"......!!"

I couldn't face them any longer. A powerful jolt of tension ran through my body, setting my arms, legs, fingers, and even my chin shaking.

The ASes were still in an uproar.

"Belle was unveiled?"

"Who unveiled her?"

"She did it herself."

"Herself?!"

"Why?!"

"What for?!"

Peggie Sue was there in the crowd. She had come to watch the moment of Belle's unveiling.

"So Belle's just an ordinary girl..." She shuddered. "Like me."

My real face might even be worse than Belle's, she thought. *In the real world, I'm a bottom-dweller without so much as a dream, but in U, I was reborn. What kind of person would throw away the dream they fought so hard to achieve?*

If I was in her shoes, I doubt I could stand it. Having my origin exposed to the whole world would be worse than standing in front of them naked.

But they say Belle revealed her own origin.

Why?

Peggie Sue couldn't make heads or tails of it.

Hiro gripped her face and shook her head.

"Now our big secret's out..."

Shinobu walked to the front of the room.

"Is this the music app?" he asked, tapping on the keyboard of the laptop sitting on a desk.

"Hey, stop!!" Hiro yelled, gripping Shinobu's arm.

He ignored her and looked up at the monitor.

"Suzu," he said, and clicked.

A SONG

The opening notes of a song drifted through the streets of U.

I stood alone in the throngs of ASes, facing into the wind. But although the wind blew against me, I did not waver in the slightest.

"Sing, Suzu," Shinobu said.

"She can't!! Not as her ordinary self!" Hiro said, tugging his arm violently.

"Yes, she can."

"There's no way!"

Ms. Kita held her breath. "Suzu," she said.

Ruka was next.

"Suzu!"

Ms. Okumoto still looked stern.

"What's she going to do?" she wondered aloud.

"Suzu," Ms. Yoshitani said, looking at me tensely.

Still looking at my feet, I began to sing.

"She sang!" Ms. Nakai said, lunging forward.

"The same girl who can't sing in public! She did it!" Ms. Hatanaka exclaimed.

My voice was barely a whisper. As I sang, still as a statue with its face downturned, oval bands encircled me. The lyrics were streaming in different languages.

Light glimmers in a flower
Like jewels in a dream
The sky breathes life, love to everything

I barely managed to sing a single verse. Looking up was impossible, so I turned my back to the crowd.

I could hear them rustling and whispering behind me.

The latest on Belle was splashed over online news sites.

Belle Unveiled!

An Idol's Origin Revealed

The Surprising Truth Behind Belle

AS comment bubbles were exploding all over the place.

Did you see her?

Belle was—

Unveiled?

No way!

Belle's real identity?

Who is she?!

Huge vertical screens popped up around me, creating an impromptu stage. The face I'd tried to keep hidden was projected on them in painstaking detail.

There was no place to hide.

I steeled my nerves and turned back toward the crowd.

Twilight was deepening over the streets of U.

At times I've thought "I'm not enough"
The chains that tie my heart
But there's still a path that lies ahead for you and I

My voice wasn't strong enough. But I kept singing anyway, my eyes closed, and when I finished, I looked down again.

The ASes watched me projected from all angles on the screens, dumbfounded.

She's shaking...

They could see my mouth trembling.

That's definitely Belle's voice, but...

She doesn't seem confident.

Hate to say it, she's so nerdy looking that it hurts

Nooo, stop destroying my fantasy

She should've stayed as Belle

My feeble self was splashed all over the screens.

Why'd she get unveiled, anyway?

I told you, she did it herself.

There were all sorts of theories about me.

Why would she reveal her own identity?

She must have a reason.

You mean she had no choice?

Then what's her reason?

Why'd she do it?

The ASes stared at the screens, flabbergasted. I kept looking at my feet.

Peggie Sue watched the unveiled Belle worriedly. She heard some young cat-eared girls talking behind her.

"Figures."

"I knew it."

"I feel sorry for her."

"God, she's so frumpy."

They turned to one another and laughed cruelly. That irritated Peggie Sue. These girls had no idea what life was like. She wanted to tell them to get lost. She probably would have thought the same thing as them a little while ago. Why did she feel so angry now?

"Belle, don't let them say whatever they want about you…"

Memories fade away, clouds of yesterday
With no one to love
is this life worth living?

A spotlight lit me up. I lifted my face, placed my hands on my chest, and sang.

Come back to me, and stay by my side
I feel my heart shake
Come, ease this ache

I'm standing over here, reaching for you
A million miles away, come back and stay

Every single AS was listening in shock. Monsters and beautiful women, dogs and cats, ducks, tough guys, hot guys, wrestlers, fairies and sages, ocean creatures and mountain creatures, knights in armor and snipers; some in witch hats or with stars painted on their faces, others with pigtails; mermaids, sirens—all of them.

No matter how far
the memories may be
When I close my eyes,
you're all that I see

Come back to me
A million miles away, come back and stay

As I finished the song, the spotlight went out. U was just entering nighttime mode, and the lights of the buildings overhead switched off in unison. Darkness descended on all of U.

A roar of applause thundered through the night.

She's our Belle after all!

That was Belle, no doubt about it!!

I feel like she was singing to someone.

Yeah, I think you're right

Some special person among the billions on U.

The screens behind me went dark one or two at a time.

Guess she just had to get it off her chest

Feels like she's been singing to one person from the start.

Eventually, the last screen went out, and darkness engulfed me.

Yeah, I remember feeling so happy thinking she was singing to me.

Me too...

So do I...

I wonder who she was really singing to.

Wish I knew.

Yeah, who could it be?

In the gaps between the units on the horizon of nighttime mode,

I saw a U-shaped moon slowly rising. I gazed into the distance as the wind swirled around me, remembering a day long ago.

"Help!! Help me!!"

The little girl's sobs reached us on the riverbank. The river had swelled in the span of mere minutes, leaving her stranded on the sandbank. The grown-ups were talking among themselves.

"This is awful!"

"We have to save her!"

"No, don't go in!"

"Why not?!"

"You'll drown trying to save her!"

"Then what should we do?!"

The girl was only four or five. Younger than me. She was wearing fancy clothes, like she came from the city, and was screaming helplessly. The grown-ups were shouting now.

"Throw her a life preserver to grab onto!"

"She's too little! She'll never catch it!"

"The police should send a rescue team!"

"They won't make it in time!"

"Then what can we do?!"

"What can we do?!"

"What now?!"

Shinobu heard their shouts, too. He glanced over and saw my mom. He said she looked unsure what to do. But she still ran forward, grabbed one of the red life jackets from the tourist canoes, and swiftly pulled it on.

I tugged on the hem of her shirt, trying desperately to keep her from going.

"Don't go, Mommy!! Don't go!!"

She squatted down and took my hand.

"I have to. If I don't, that little girl will die."

Now I remembered—that was what she said.

She stood up, shook me off, and ran toward the water. I tried to chase after her but stumbled and fell. I stood up and screamed at her as loudly as I could.

"Mommy!! Mommy!! Mommy!!"

She didn't look back. Her gaze fixed on the girl, she entered the water upstream and rode the current down to her.

A light rain began to fall.

The little girl was rescued from the river. The men pulled her out and all the grown-ups ran over to her.

"Hurry, hurry!"

"Is she okay?!"

"Call an ambulance!"

"Quick!"

"Hurry up!"

I stared at them, the rain soaking me.

"Stay strong!"

"They'll be here any minute!"

"You made it!"

"It's a miracle!"

"Thank goodness!"

The little girl was wearing the red life jacket. The one Mom should have been wearing.

The instant I noticed it, I understood what was happening.

My mom wasn't there.

"Mommy… Mommy… Mommy!!"

I screamed for her over and over, but she was nowhere to be found. I heard an ambulance siren far away. The little girl was wrapped in a blanket and carried away from the riverbank by a crowd of grown-ups. Everyone was so focused on the little girl that they didn't notice my mom was gone.

"Mommy!!"

I was the only one who kept screaming for her.

Over. And over. And over.

As the rain pattered down, the river picked up speed.

Just then, I noticed something.

"...Huh?!"

Mom was on the far bank.

The roar of the river seemed to go silent.

"Mo—"

I tried to say her name but couldn't. Instead, tears and snot poured from my eyes and nose.

Mom was staring at me from the far bank.

She was smiling. Why was she smiling? It was the same smile she had when we played together.

I could hardly see through my tears.

"Don't go...!!"

Don't leave me alone.

I can't make it on my own.

I tottered forward.

Step by step, I walked unsteadily over the riverbank stones. I headed toward the rushing river as if it were pulling me in.

"Suzu!"

Just then, a small hand grabbed my own and pulled me back.

It was Shinobu.

The roar of the river returned to my ears.

* * *

Then there was the other scene I always remembered.

Shinobu with a mini basketball in his hand, squatting beside me as I cried and peering into my face.

That place still exists. It's right next to the playground monkey bars at the old elementary school.

Shinobu looked out the window of the second-floor classroom.

"I'm not her dad, and I'm not one of her girlfriends," he said. "But I don't think it hurts for you to have another person worrying about you."

Ruka put her hand over her mouth like the pieces had just come together for her. "So that's how her mom..."

"You're not the only one, Shinobu." Ms. Okumoto's eyes misted over in reminiscence.

"We always tried to fill her mom's shoes," Ms. Nakai said, fixing him with a wistful gaze.

"We laughed and got mad and cried—just like her mom would have." Ms. Kita looked down, smiling.

"What a lousy bunch of moms we are." Ms. Hatanaka was wiping away a tear.

"Suzu has brought us so much joy," Ms. Yoshitani said, her hand on her chest and her eyes glistening.

Other than the moonlight, the streets of U were black as ink. I squinted into the darkness.

"Kei...where are you? Answer me... Let me hear your voice... Kei... Kei, are you there...?!"

My feelings became a song. There were no words, only my voice tracing a melody.

"La la la la la la, la la la la la, la la la la la la..."

A faint light glowed in my chest. At first it was a tiny point in the very middle, but as I sang, it grew bigger. Quietly spreading from inside to out, the light shone like a candle burning in my chest.

I remembered experiencing this light before, back when I'd been crying outside the Dragon's door. My arms had been crossed over my chest, and when I opened them, there was a round, bruise-like mark on my chest. The mark emitted a soft, warm light.

This was the same. U's body-sharing technology was giving my heartbreak a visible form.

The more I sang, the stronger the light became.

"Suzu...!" Ms. Hatanaka's AS gasped when she saw it.

"Suzu, you...," Ms. Okumoto murmured.

The choir ladies were in U as ASes. The lovely, colorful costumes they each wore suited them perfectly.

"Suzu...!"

Ruka and Kamishin were there, too. Ruka's AS was a bluebird holding an alto sax. Kamishin's was a dog carrying a big canoe on his back.

I kept singing.

"La la la la la la, la la la la la, la la la la la la..."

I saw a tear fall from one AS's eye. It wasn't what I'd have expected from his fierce expression.

"La la la la la la, la la la la la, la la la la la la..."

Some of the ASes had lights in their chests like me. I saw one, then two, then three in the dark. Soon there were more, the light rippling outward from one chest to another.

Dozens, then hundreds, then thousands.

The lights pulsed emotionally in rhythm with my breath as I sang. Feelings without words. Like sorrow, like encouragement, like comfort for sadness, like hands lifting me up.

Hiro's AS looked at the lights. "I was your only friend… And now…look at you!"

She was crying, her chest glowing.

The web of lights rippled out to the horizon.

Tens of thousands. Hundreds of thousands. Millions.

The light in each of those chests was only a gentle, soft, modest glow. But together, they shone powerfully, resiliently, confidently.

"La la la la la la, la la la la la, la la la la la la…"

I gazed out at the dizzying sea of lights.

Tens of millions. Hundreds of millions.

What an incredible sight.

All these people were gathered together, their feelings taking form before my eyes. Feelings were no longer invisible. Here in U, here in our chests, they had shape and color and brightness.

"……!"

The thought brought my own feelings surging irrepressibly upward. Tears blinded my vision and my jaw trembled so bad I could hardly sing. Holding back sobs, I looked down and managed to wipe my tears with one hand, which caused me to stop singing. I shook my head and switched to the other hand. I still couldn't keep singing.

"Suzu!!" the choir members' ASes yelled, the lights in their chests pulsating.

"Suzu!" Ruku's AS cried, holding up her sax as her chest glowed.

Peggie Sue was there, too.

"Belle!!" she shouted, filling me with still more emotion. "Keep singing!! Don't stop!!"

She began singing loudly in my place.

"La la la la la la!"

The ASes nearby stared in confusion.

"It's Peggie Sue."

"*That* Peggie Sue?"

"What's she doing here?"

She ignored them and screamed, "Belle!! Sing!!"

That seemed to set off the other ASes. They picked up my broken melody and started to sing as well.

"La la la la la la, la la la la la, la la la la la la..."

Little by little, the melody spread. The sea of ASes were singing my wordless song together. Their voices rose from the farthest corners of the park.

"La la la la la la, la la la la la, la la la la la la..."

The choir ASes were swaying and singing, too. Ruka's AS was playing the melody on her sax. It was a magnificent jam session of the masses. Innumerable ASes were together in song, their chests glowing in the dark. And the more they sang, the brighter their lights shone.

"Wh-what's happening?!" Justin stuttered as he watched, white as a ghost. "She was unveiled—so why is she still here?!"

He hadn't expected this. Once a person's been unveiled, they can't live in U anymore. That's what makes unveiling so powerful. Those with the power to unveil control the world.

Belle had definitely been unveiled. He'd thought the whole world had mocked her, jeered her, and hurled her to the ground. So what was he looking at now? It was all wrong. What had happened?

One of the sponsor logos behind him drifted away.

"Hey!" he cried, whipping his head around to look. The other logos started disappearing, too, like a receding tide. In mere minutes, he had lost all his sponsors.

"Damn!!" Justin muttered, clenching his teeth. He looked hounded. He was no longer a person of power, no longer a chosen AS. The millions of ASes with their glowing chests appeared before him like a golden ocean. Suddenly, its center swelled high into the air.

"Wh-what's going on?!"

An enormous whale encrusted with speakers was surfacing leisurely through the golden sea, raising a huge wave.

It opened its gargantuan mouth and roared, as if to join in the song. Water jetted from its blowhole, glittering in the air like fireworks.

The whale's enormous rostrum lifted me with it. I was in the same place where Belle, dressed in a gown of red flowers, had boldly sung to the world. I was standing in the same spot, as my real self.

Standing and singing boldly.

Surrounded by its offspring, the whale floated leisurely over the golden sea.

Sing, let your heart soar!
Sing forever!
Sad and so happy! Feelings flow over, now
Our world is full of all kinds of colors
Closing my eyes I can still see the stars
Shine in the sky, sing in their harmony
Flowers, they're blooming, oh it's beautiful!

I wasn't a beautiful woman, not by any stretch of the imagination. I was just a freckled kid from the countryside. But Belle was inside me.

The other me gave me strength. Belle had disappeared, but she remained inside me, as my core. Living as Belle had made me stronger.

Thank you.

The instant those words rose in my mind, countless flowers blossomed from my body. Unending bunches of them adorned the streets of U. They fluttered down from the drifting whale and settled on the glowing ASes.

The whale and its babies swam languidly through the golden sea of swaying ASes. A U-shaped moon hovered in the sky above.

I belted out the last lines of the song, like I was embracing all the life that existed in that moment.

Kei watched the performance in awe.

"Wow…!"

Tears were streaming from Tomo's eyes.

"Kei, I…I want to see Belle… I wanna see her."

But Kei was unsure, still suspicious.

"…Is she really Belle, though? I don't totally trust her yet."

Then, seeming to make up his mind, he whispered, "But…"

If Tomo said he wanted to see her—

REAL FACES

I slowly raised my head. A moment ago, I'd been in U, but now I was back in the abandoned classroom. My head was as fuzzy as if I'd woken from a dream. In front of me was the same disconnected video chat window. Then a NOW LOADING message appeared and the connection was restored. I heard Tomo's voice through the speaker.

"Belle…? Can you see us?"

Tomo's and Kei's faces were peering into their laptop's webcam. They had reopened our chat.

"Whoo-hoooo!!"

Cheers erupted in the small crowd gathered at the school. Everyone was jumping around and shouting joyfully. Only I was in a dreamlike daze.

"Suzu?" Shinobu said.

I looked up.

"Your feelings got through to them," he said, smiling. His smile brought me back to reality. My heart danced with joy.

"Shinobu, I'm so happy!" I said and hugged him like a little kid. He hugged me back, patting my head.

"I know."

I rubbed my teary cheek on him.

"I'm so glad..."

Kei and Tomo's father heard a notification ping on his phone.

"...Hmm?" he muttered, looking down from his remote meeting to check it. He'd received a message with a video attached. He pressed PLAY.

On the screen, a vase toppled onto the floor and shattered.

"Why don't you ever listen to me?"

It was him.

"What the hell is this?"

Someone was spreading the video around. He frowned and strode out of his room.

"Write this down. Our address is—"

Just as Kei was about to tell us where he lived over the chat, the door to his room flew open with a *bang* and his father walked in.

"*Hey!*" Kei and Tomo shouted, turning to look at him. Their father glanced around the room and spotted the laptop webcam.

"*So that's what you used!*" he said, heading straight for it.

Kei stood up from his chair and tried to intercept his father.

"Stop... Stop!!"

He desperately pushed away his father's hands as they reached for the camera. Tomo jumped into the fray, too, but without success.

"*Move!*" their father shouted, shoving away the two squatting children like they were inanimate objects. His terrifying face leered into the camera.

"*You damn brats!!*" he shouted, reaching out like he was going to grab us through the screen.

He slammed the laptop shut. The same instant, an error message appeared.

An error occurred. Please try again later.

The connection was cut again.

"......!!"

All we could do was gape in shock. The choir members began whispering to one another.

"...I'm worried about those boys."

"We've got to go protect them."

"But where are they?"

"They didn't get to tell us."

Ruka interrupted haltingly. "I think I might know."

"You do?!"

"I heard the evening chime playing in the background."

"You could hear it over all that noise?"

Ruka looked down like she was replaying it in her head. "First was 'The Sunset Glow' and then 'The Coconut.'"

"Those are standard songs that towns play at five," Shinobu said right away.

"But two?" Ms. Nakai asked, looking at him.

"They must live on the border of two towns, where you can hear both."

"Which two towns?" Ms. Yoshitani asked.

"I'll look it up." Shinobu took out his phone to search.

"I was able to pull up the recording!" Hiro said from her seat at a desk.

"Oooh, show us!" the choir members said, gathering around the big screen.

The image showed Kei's chat screen at the moment the

connection was cut. Hiro rewound until it showed Kei crouched beneath his father. Then she hit PLAY.

Outside the white room, two melodies were playing. "The Sunset Glow" and "The Coconut," just like Ruka had said.

"There it is!" cried Ms. Nakai, sounding impressed.

"Great ears, Ruka," Kamishin added.

Suddenly, Ms. Okumoto pointed to the edge of the screen. "What's that outside the window?"

"Where?"

She noticed something out there.

"Enlarge it."

Hiro zoomed in.

"What is that?"

As she corrected the image quality of the overexposed window, details emerged.

"An office building? An apartment complex?"

"Two of them?"

Two identical high-rises were clearly visible outside the window. Ms. Nakai shook Hiro's shoulders.

"Where?! Keep searching!"

"How?? This isn't enough to go on!"

There was no way to identify the buildings. Just then, Kamishin leaned toward the screen with his hand shading his eyes.

"...Huh? Hold up," he muttered.

"What?" Ruka asked, looking at him. He thought for a few seconds, then pointed to the screen.

"Ruka, I know where this is."

"No way!" Hiro shouted, turning around.

"Wait a sec, I'm trying to remember."

Kamishin casually began searching on his phone.

"Hurry up!!" Hiro shouted. She sounded irritated.

Meanwhile, Shinobu had come up with an answer. "Got it!"

Hiro swiveled back to her keyboard. "Where?"

"There's five places near Tokyo. The only one with high-rises is in between Ota Ward and Kawasaki!"

Hiro pulled up a map. The viewpoint jumped from our location on the Niyodo River, over the rest of Kochi Prefecture, and then east to Tokyo. Finally it zoomed in on the Tama River running between Ota and Kawasaki.

Kamishin jerked his face up.

"I found it! Look!"

He thrust out his phone. On the screen was a group picture with him striking a pose in the center of the front row. It was the same one he'd shown us before. Behind him, on the other side of the Tama River, were two identical tall buildings.

The map shifted to a 3D view. As Hiro circled us around Musashi-Kosugi, the same two identical buildings appeared. She compared them to the image captured from the live chat and the picture Kamishin had AirDropped her.

"All three match. It's a go!"

Shinobu and Kamishin gave each other a high five.

"Nice one!"

Ruka and Hiro high-fived, too.

"We did it!!"

Ms. Yoshitani was politely placing a phone call. "Hello? So sorry to bother you, but there are two children in immediate need of protection in the location I'm about to describe."

She was talking to the child welfare office. But her face quickly clouded over.

"What? You can't go right away? Rules? Forty-eight hours?"

There seemed to be a rule stating the agency must check on the children's condition within 48 hours.

"But what if something happens in the meantime?"

I turned toward her. "I have to go!!"

My body took off running on its own.

"Suzu!"

"We'll drive you to the station!"

Ms. Nakai and Ms. Kita ran after me.

"Suzu!" Shinobu called.

I flew out of the classroom. I didn't have time to answer.

The engine of Ms. Kita's Daihatsu Move Canbus started up with a purr and the headlights clicked on. White smoke puffed from the tailpipe as she swiveled the car around in the schoolyard then sped away from the old school.

We had about half an hour until sundown. Ms. Kita gripped the steering wheel and raced down the highway along the Niyodo. From the passenger seat, Ms. Nakai reached back to where I was sitting and showed me the information on routes to Tokyo that she'd pulled up on her phone.

"It's too late to catch a flight," she said.

Ms. Kita threw her a worried glance. "So…she's going straight to Tokyo?"

They dropped me at Ino Station, where the limited express Ashizuri 16 was leaving on time at 7:15 PM. They saw me off from the platform.

"Think she'll be okay by herself?"

"It was her own decision."

They really did sound like moms.

The Ashizuri 16 arrived on Platform 2 at Kochi Station at 7:28 PM. The sun was already down, the sky a bluish-black.

The bus bound for Tokyo Disneyland Bus Terminal West left Kochi Bus Terminal at 8:10 PM and headed north on the Kochi Expressway.

The world outside the windows was pitch-black. I watched dots of light in the towns scroll slowly into the distance. I knew Dad must've been worried about me not coming home. Thinking about it made my chest tighten up. I tapped out a message to him on my phone.

Dad, I didn't say anything before I left, but I'm going on a kind of long trip.

I got a notification that he'd read my text, then a few minutes later, an answer:

The choir ladies messaged me.

So they'd already let him know. That was a relief.

Sorry for always doing whatever I feel like, I wrote.

I'm sure you have your reasons.

Someone I care about is in trouble

And you're trying to help them.

I don't know if I'll be able to though.

I couldn't remember the last time I'd spoken so openly to Dad.

You've been so sad and lonely ever since your mom died. But you stuck it out. I know it wasn't easy, but you've grown into such a kind young woman. You understand what other people are going through.

My chest tightened further.

Suzu, your mother raised you, and that's why you're such a good person.

I could sense the warmth in his words. My vision got so blurry I could hardly read.

Now go be a good person to that friend of yours!

Teardrops splashed onto my phone screen.

Thanks, I answered.

The next morning at 6:15, the bus pulled into Yokohama City Air Terminal. I transferred to the Toyoko railway line, and by 7, I was walking through the ticket gates at Tamagawa Station.

Outside the station, raindrops were starting to spatter the pavement. I looked around with growing anxiety. I'd never been to this station before. The streets and buildings were all unfamiliar. Would I be able to find them?

I started running through the light rain.

I sprinted uphill with the Tama River at my back. Houses bigger than any I'd seen in Kochi sat in dignified rows behind ginkgo trees. The street was abandoned. Every now and then, a large car drove quietly past.

I stopped at an intersection and looked around. I was overwhelmed with the fear that I'd get myself lost. Finding the right house among all of them felt absurd. I started running again, hoping to shake off my unease.

Panting, I stopped at a corner next to a luxury condo and took another look around. Ripples spread across a puddle. The rain was falling harder now.

"Huff… Huff…"

I felt my energy draining away as I peered anxiously at my surroundings. My arms hung limply by my sides from exhaustion. I was never going to help him at this rate. I had to find him, and fast…

As that thought crossed my mind, I stumbled.

"Ah!!"

I fell forward on the wet sidewalk. I lay there moaning, momentarily unable to move. Planting my hands on the ground, I lifted my aching body and wiped my wet, muddy face with the back of my hand. I had to keep going. I clenched my teeth and started running again, my eyes trained ahead of me.

I finally found them. On the far side of the hill lined with mansions, across the Tama River, I saw the two high-rise buildings.

"There they are!" I blurted out.

The buildings were unmistakable. Which meant…

"Belle…?" a voice called from the top of the hill.

"…Huh?!"

I turned around. A small figure was standing in the street without an umbrella.

"You…came?"

It was Tomo, wearing a white hoodie.

"Tomo!"

"…Belle…!"

I started racing up the hill toward him like I was defying gravity. He ran toward me, hood up and arms outstretched. We met in the middle and hugged. His skin was so white it was nearly translucent. I was surprised by how thin he was. This frail boy clung to me, seeking my help.

"It's okay," I murmured, wrapping my arm around his back soothingly. "Everything is okay now."

Watching suspiciously from the top of the hill was another boy—Kei.

"Are you really Belle?" he called.

I smiled up at him, still hugging Tomo. Kei walked slowly toward us. But midway down, he stopped and stayed there at a slight distance. I hadn't yet gained his trust. How could I close the gap? Rain kept on falling between us.

"Hey! Where'd you two go?!"

The door to one of the fancy houses at the top of the hill was open. Their father walked out of it, yelling.

"Tomo! Kei!! Where are you?!"

Kei flinched and looked over his shoulder. His father rounded a curve and came into view.

"Kei!! Why did you go outside without my permission?!"

He strode toward us imposingly. Kei's face stiffened. He backed away from his father as if he were being pushed by an invisible force.

"......!!"

Without thinking, I pulled both boys close and turned protectively away from their father.

"Who the hell are you?!" he yelled, grabbing my shoulder violently. "You're the one who wrote those things online, aren't you?!"

Once he jumped to that conclusion, anger colored his face. He shook my shoulder. I kept my arms tight around Kei and Tomo, looked at the ground, and didn't move.

"Child abuse?! That's a damn lie!" he screamed indignantly.

I sensed from his tone that he really did find the notion outrageous. Maybe he believed he was acting as a parent should. Maybe he believed that even as he made Kei's and Tomo's lives miserable.

I had to protect them. I tightened my grip around their shoulders. Kei gasped and looked up at me.

"I know this feeling...," he mumbled, like he was remembering something.

"Kei! Tomo! Get back in the house! Do you hear me?! Listen to your father!"

The rain beat down harder. Their father gripped my shoulder and pulled again and again. I sat down on the ground, still embracing Kei and Tomo.

"Dammit, girl! Are you trying to destroy our family?!"

His claw-like fingers clutched my head and face, shaking me back and forth like a rag doll. Then he dug in his nails and dragged them upward. There was a horrifying scraping sound—the nail on his middle finger was carving out the flesh of my left cheek. A second later, pain shot through me.

"I won't let you do it! Never!!"

He raised his fist menacingly.

I couldn't protect them like this. I steeled my nerves, then quietly stood and turned toward him, making my body into a shield.

"......?!"

He had his fist still raised, his eyes widening in surprise.

I stood like a silent wall between him and the two boys, doing nothing to protect myself. I simply took him in with an unwavering gaze.

Rain poured down.

He must not have expected me to act like that, because he flinched and suddenly went limp. But then, his hatred seeming to surge again, he raised his fist and shook it threateningly.

"See this?!" he bellowed.

I think he must've lived his whole life looking down on people that way, forcing them to do what he wanted. He looked genuinely prepared to punch me. I stayed still, my eyes fixed on his. A rivulet of blood ran down my left cheek.

I refuse to let you look down on my spirit.

I noticed something shift in him. His fist seemed to weaken, like the strength had left it, and his arm began to shake. He was shaking like he couldn't control his own body. He must have realized what was happening, because I could see him force the strength back into his hand.

"...See this?!" he thundered again, waving his fist around.

Rainwater flowed from my hair down my cheek, mixing with blood before it pooled beneath my jaw and fell in droplets.

I will not let you look down on me.

I kept staring unwaveringly up at him.

"......Agh... Aghhh!"

He seemed unable to bring his fist down on me. The shaking spread from his arm to his entire body. He staggered backward and collapsed onto the ground like his strength had abandoned him. He looked up weakly, his hair plastered to his forehead by the rain. He was no longer a grown-up or a parent, but merely a feeble, miserable man.

"Aghhh... Aghhhh...!"

Then, as if he could no longer stand to be there, he scooted backward, twisted around onto his knees, and disappeared up the hill like a man on the run.

I watched him silently. The rain had faded to a drizzle.

"...Belle," I heard Kei say.

"......?"

He stood up and looked at me blankly.

"When you were holding me a minute ago, I finally knew. You really are Belle..."

His expression was still blank; it seemed he didn't know how to express the emotions inside him.

"Thanks for coming. I...I really wanted you to come."

I think it took every bit of courage he had to say that. I think he really did want me to come. I could sense it in his words.

"I wanted to meet you, Belle."

He smiled awkwardly. I felt my body fill with warmth.

"Me too," I said. I stepped forward and hugged him. We pressed our foreheads together like a couple. He gazed at me with gentle eyes.

"When I saw you standing up to him, I realized—I have to stand up to him, too. I'm gonna fight back."

I closed my eyes, reflecting on everything that had happened.

"You taught me something, too," I said. "You set my timid spirit free."

He blushed innocently, back to being the fourteen-year-old boy he was.

"...Thank you. I love you, Belle."

Tomo got unsteadily to his feet and said, "Belle, you...are beautiful," while gazing at me.

He'd said the same thing to me another time. I stood there covered in dirt and blood, filled with pride and happiness at his words.

"Thank you," I said.

The three of us hugged as a gentle rain doused us.

Today, like every day, U is packed with people from all corners of the world.

Someone is visiting for the first time, falteringly registering an account, full of expectations and fears.

Maybe that someone is you.

An automated voice is speaking.

"U is another reality. Your AS is another you. You can't redo life in the real world. But in U, you can."

A U-shaped moon slowly rises.

"It's time to live as another you. It's time to begin a new life. It's time to change the world."

* * *

I left Tokyo and arrived at Kochi Station in the afternoon. By the time the train for Susaki arrived at Ino Station, the sun was low in the sky.

I climbed down onto the platform. As the train pulled away, I saw Dad standing on the platform across the track.

I stared at him. He stared at me.

I had a big bandage on my left cheek. He was probably wondering what had happened. Maybe he was wondering if I'd gotten myself into something dangerous. Maybe he wanted to ask me what happened.

"...What about dinner tonight?" he said.

At first, I was caught off guard by the unexpected but at the same time totally ordinary question. Then I smiled.

"Sounds great," I replied. He smiled, too.

"Let's have tataki, then," he said.

That was the end of our first in-person conversation in a long time. How many months had it taken us to manage this tiny exchange? How many years? But I didn't care. We'd finally managed to say it: *What about dinner? Sounds great.* We'd finally achieved that tiny thing. I savored the weight of those words that took so long to say. Then I smiled, fully refreshed.

"It's good to be back," I said.

"Welcome home." Dad returned a smile.

We exchanged relieved glances. Just then—

"Suzu!!"

—I heard Ms. Nakai calling to me from outside the station building. The choir ladies, Hiro, Ruka, Kamishin, and Shinobu had all come to meet me.

"Welcome back!!" they yelled.

* * *

We walked home slowly along the banks of the Niyodo River as the setting sun tinted the water. The choir ladies were up front and Dad brought up the rear. Hiro and Ruka were chatting like old friends behind me. Kamishin watched them, smiling.

I strolled alongside Shinobu.

"…Suzu?" he said.

"Yeah?"

"It was pretty impressive the way you went and protected those kids."

I glanced over at him. He gave me a long look, then smiled.

"You were amazing."

I looked up at him in a daze, feeling my cheeks flushing. Shinobu stretched his arms over his head, still walking.

"I'm finally free," he said, looking up at the sky. "I don't have to protect you anymore. I can just be by your side. I've wanted that for a while now."

For the first time, I realized that was how he'd been feeling. I didn't know what to say, so I gazed up at the same sky he was looking at. The sun was setting behind a cumulonimbus in the west. The golden cloud against the blue sky was bracing, invigorating.

Shinobu stopped and stared up at it. So did Hiro, Ruka, and Kamishin. Then Dad and the choir ladies did, too. Sunbeams shone beautifully from the top of the towering billows. My eyes still fixed on the sky, I silently apologized to Shinobu.

No, that's not right.

What I needed to say to him was "thank you." I hoped that one day I'd be able to say it to him out loud. I wanted to become the kind of person who could say that.

A gentle breeze ruffled my hair. I heard the choir ladies having a discussion.

"Why don't we all sing something while we're walking?"

"Good idea. We can get some practice in."

"The fall concert is coming up, you know."

"What should we sing?"

"*That* song, of course!"

"Right, of course."

They looked back at me.

"Suzu, you take the lead!" Ms. Yoshiya said.

"Yeah, sing!" Hiro, Ruka, and Kamishin piled on eagerly.

I glanced over at Shinobu in surprise.

"I'm listening," he said with a grin.

"...Okay!" I looked ahead, smiled, and took a deep breath. "Here I go!!"